Cities of India

Cities of India

Steve Noyes

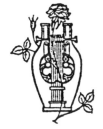

Ekstasis Editions

© Steve Noyes, 1994

Canadian Cataloguing in Publication Data

Noyes, Steve
    Cities of India

    Fiction.
    ISBN 0-921215-79-7

    I. Title.
    PS8577.O96C57 1994   C813'.54   C94-910584-8
    PR9199.3.N69C57 1994

Cover Painting: "Waking Fire," by Miles Lowry
Design: Richard Olafson

Acknowledgements:

The author would like to express his appreciation to the following individuals who have made invaluable contributions to this book: Eva Caputa, Warren Carter, Al and Eurithe Purdy, John Orser, Sue Donaldson, the staff of the George and the Dragon, Mustafa Yölücü, Shukran Wassalaam, Maty Appaya, and Kim Stewart.

Published in 1994 by
Ekstasis Editions Canada Ltd.   **Ekstasis Editions**
Box 8474, Main Postal Outlet   Box 571
Victoria, B.C. V8W 3S1   Banff, Alberta T0L 0C0

Cities of India has been published with the generous financial assistance of the The Canada Council.

Printed in Canada by Hignell Printing Ltd., Winnipeg, Manitoba

In Memoriam Lansing Craig Piprell, 1954-94

"I held it truth, with he who sings
  To one clear harp in diverse tones
That men may rise on stepping stones
  Of their dead selves to higher things."
   ——Tennyson

 For C.

ياعـدو مـــالك من شـــوقٍ و أراق

و مر الطـــيـــفِ من أهـــوال طارق

ya: idu ma laka min shawqin wa iraaqi
wa marra al-Tayf'in min ahwaali Taariqi

O hardened one, who is to match you for wandering and nightmare
And the terrors of a traveller, the coming of a spectre.
                    —Ta'abbat ash'sharran

Contents

A Winter

Whenever I return to Winnipeg, which

is usually in the winter, it doesn't much interest me; it's all grey over trolley wires and such; the downtown stores are grubbily hung with their Christmas lights; shopping in an underground concourse; heavy coats; it is a lot to get through, and then get the hell out. But before I do, another thing always happens. I get thinking about an uncle—I've never seen him—got his face ripped off by a barbwire fence on a snowmobile. I hear his voice, though, Fred's. I imagine him gripping a coffee cup, all recovered, but his son, after all, dead.

I was brought up in Saint Vital. You follow the Red River to get to it. The suburbs. My parents got a split level and not much of a yard near about a million and a half convenience stores, Seven Elevens and Mac's Milks.

If it's not too cold, November, say, we sit in parkas on the deck they built and have a chat. They are not that old. Dad looks okay in his beard. Well, a lot better than Mom would. "Our house, you know what it is? It's sinking, holy doodle," is what she says.

Dad says he's got engineers, good guys, who've got documents say it isn't.

"We're selling," he says. "If someone buys it," she.

"So you don't know yet."

They've got a barbecue out front but no bird feeder. Winnipeggers are supposed to have bird feeders. This is close to the heart of what a Winnipegger is; they think this modest ability to attract hungry birds to their homes is a great talent, and they love the birds, at least until spring, when they begin hollering at them like they were pests.

"So what's Vancouver like?"

I tell my Dad. Mom isn't listening. She gets up and walks over to the fence. Neither of us are surprised at her behaviour; she once told us in the kitchen she could do things with her mind, like go off and hide in it.

"What sort of things?" I had asked.

"Oh," she said, "things."

The uncle was a short man, I could tell by his voice, and the wire at dusk had jumped straight through his face, cutting into the jawbone and tearing away with it his lips; whale-blubber sprays of fleshy blood were found well away from the running machine on the snow. The son had been beheaded.

There were not enough funds for the funeral.

And that is all I knew, all I had been told. It is hardly ever mentioned.

That winter I had worked, instead of gone to school, in Saint Boniface near the Lagimodière tracks. I started early in the morning cold and black and there were boxcars a mile long and I had to climb between the couplings, jump them and up again, sometimes freights rolling with unshaken snow down the middle track slow and it was easy to outrun them, and the watchmen I avoided. I never made it in on time.

"More coffee?" my Dad says.

You can see the crack he's talking about from the inside, sure, it runs from the living room, which is sunken, along the ceiling into the kitchen and the dining room, a good inch thick...

I am cutting red ends on the saw. Near the doors, before coffee break. Hands red and cold. A crank, then a banging crank, the door is lifting and I see Donny and I shut the saw off. When Donny comes in that is my signal, I shut the saw off and listen to the shrill whine of its teeth, he comes in with the forklift. He stamps and baffs his earmuffs, then presses the gizmo to close the door. The lift sits clicking monstrous on its forks, cooling off.

"Here you go," he says, and he slips me the baggie in his glove to my pocket.

"You wanna?"

"Upstairs? Sure. Why not?"

We pull out the chairs in the lunchroom.

"That was easy to get."

"Thanks."

"I can get more."

"*Qui le roule bamboule*," I say.

"What's that, French?"

"French."

"Forget it, I'll roll."

He rolls, twists, smacks his lips.

Lights up.

Big fucking grin.

"Old lady's getting a better job. She's right up there in the bank. Train her an' everything. Matches. I got some. All fucking right."

"Yeah."

"We're rolling in it."

"Good smoke."

11

"You want I can get some more," says Donny.

His eyes are points, red, widening.

"You think we did a good job on this lunchroom?"

"Yeah, excellent."

I did not like to talk to Donny when stoned.

"You think so?" He looks around at first the west wall, then the south, then the east, then north, where I am. The room took us two months; we were stoned the whole time we worked on it. That plywood looks like it's been sawed with a kid's saw. He peers at the paint. Wipes his nose on his scarf. Donny, a real steeplehead in his own way—.

"Did I ever tell you how I lost my license?"

"One or two times."

"I dunno, this room really bugs me. Picks my ass. Well," and he slaps the table, not hard, "get back at her."

When I get down start the saw up, he's drifted outdoors again with the lift, just taking it around and around the yard, touring all the lumber we're supposed to count when we got time. Donny may not own the place, but he looks like he does and that's about it.

Over the red ends Big Jim's face appears.

"Psst. Hey! There's Indians working here, d'you know?"

He is Indian. I smile at him.

"If you smile yer an asshole."

He shoots nails at me every morning, after coffee.

I took the bus home in the last of the lime yellow sun far off in the pale snow near Lagimodière Boulevard, the last of the sun red on the mint, a new national one, a pyramid made of glass that glinted and glinted. When I saw yellow grass between myself and the pyramid I quit. That was April.

Fred had shown up at my grandparents', after the big Christmas dinner Grandma put on. We were all in armchairs in the living room, stuffy; Grandad was holding forth. He had a legitimate grievance: my grandmother, still puttering about the kitchen with her glasses on the tip of her nose, had been fired. The son of a bitch had tricked her. She had trained her boss's son for her own job, and the boss's son got the job and she got the boot. It was simple as that. We heard her let the man in the back door, and she called up to us, perturbed, she told us Fred, *Fred*, was here on Christmas Eve. We had the TV trays out, there was a big special on, we just sat there and Fred didn't come up, he sat with my grand-mother down in the kitchen. We could hear them talking.

Grandfather yelled, "You making coffee in there?" and Grandmother's voice came fluttering back, "did you want it with cream in it, did you?" and there was a clink of a bottle, which no one paid any attention to in the living room, and everyone forgot that the man with the mended face was there, and with us, and you see I know they were drinking down there, and I know she kissed him. And Merry Christmas.

Cities of India

The air conditioning was on high, it

hummed in the hotel room. Harry, his wife drifting to and and fro, motioned to her to sit down, conserve energy; then he was repeating a number into the phone; he had to verify it, took out his wallet. He kept his eye on Allison. He got put on hold.

"Hey," he said to her, "among the *living*? Remember?"

"The living." She said it dully.

"At least until we get out of here," he said. "I'll only be on the phone for the usual."

She had forgotten the heat (it had been inside the shell of the airplane in Bombay, and there was a hand of it behind the curtains here in the Calcutta Ramada) and the windy thin wall of a thousand window facades for the princesses of Ashiauyapur. The faces of rooms, clouds, clowns, stirred in a condition of a new world about her, a room with very few names. It was her practise to make tea in the afternoons, at tea-time, and in this way she grew attached to the shifting light. Now and then she felt the tea-steam on her face, which was dry: that was a private abhorrence of hers, that the invisible become visible in her tears, with no protection or advance warning.

Three times the busboy with his commendable cap, white shirt, and the same question, "You like to drink?" and his hand out for tip had come knocking.

Ah, she remembered the Ramada. There, elevator music in the stairs.

Otherwise she was beyond all this exhausted emotional tourism. Three times she told him to go away, and Harry had walked in from the suite's TV parlour and dismissed the boy, hanging on to his newspaper grimly, his glasses hooked down on his nose to peer better. Allison had the uncanny feeling that he was looking, or waiting for something—something to happen, perhaps, a past-altering miracle or nothing, a further collapse, standing in his slippers with the papers.

From then on they shared not a single perception; and she recognized this. They were different people. It was banal, and it was not a mood to suit them; but they found it explanatory; it had the mysterious power to explain, to anneal. Their efforts to ignore each other, however, were productions of much bungling, mornings especially. It seemed to take hours for Harry to make to the officials responsible his few phone calls and the simplest of his demands clear. When they were finished he smoked. She smoked.

Eventually the phone rang.

"Blast it, man, can't you. I——. Yes. Yes, yes."

She profoundly never wanted to meet these people.

"I see, I see, I see."

He was rubbing at his eyes.

She could not think of anything but planes and surfaces, the values and properties of objects she could operate.

They lived in a curtain. The smoke from their cigarettes disappeared, soldierly and invisible. They went up and down to meals over plush red carpets in a silent elevator.

They had to identify the body, officially, tomorrow, before its journey.

"Yes? Yes," the doctor acknowledged her quick, lidded nod. Harry came out behind her. The doctor wheeled the lock shut. Harry, struck by the size of the door, walked over and touched it.

"It used to be a furnace," said the doctor, "it was left from the British. They always overheated this hospital. They thought everything was a railway, I am telling you, all the scrap, all the rubbish, all the waste, they burned it here. Now, my assistants will be making the preparations. How will you be arranging to send, my deepest sympathy, your son home?"

"By plane," she said.

Harry told him the flight number, and then she had to search through her purse for change. To tip him.

They had landed in Bombay for only half an hour on the way in, and Mark had gone to stand at the back door, where, characteristically, Harry thought, the baggage handlers had briefly come aboard for a smoke. Mark was smoking with them close to the oval door.

Better go back and talk with them.

All they could see as they stood there, Mark in his 2 Live Crew tee-shirt, was the dark and a few airport buildings and a few billboards.

"So that's Bombay."

Fatherly. Avuncular.

"It sure is," Mark said.

Allison, when they were on Goa, weeks ago, had a Hindi song explained to her by a boy; she thought it repulsive and still does whenever she cares to think of it. As it happened the narrative concerned one of the the princesses of Ashiauyapur, Mira, who was nubile and about to be the bride in a huge arranged marriage. Mira, an unusually devout girl, upon arriving in her bridegroom's village, secludes herself in a room lit with torches and begins to pray. While the crowd sings of her husband's beauty and wisdom, she sings that there is no beauty equal, not even a zircon, to the beauty of two hands in simple prayer. She is so deep in her meditations that she appears dead. The young man hears of this and, when she does not respond to him, believes she is dead, and has her cremated. At her pyre in the great river he tells his family.

> *Asi layay lagun*
> *Mira ho gai magun.*

> *(That's how the wedding began,*
> *Mira was dead to the world.)*

The boy had paused when he said "the husband believes she was dead."

An ambiguity there. Or he did not know how to say it in English.

That, too, was possible.

Something had prevented her, she knew, from merely walking away: the descending light in the streets, then the crowd pressing in.

He and his father had argued, Harry, tired, stupid and adamant, just around the corner. Mark wanted to buy some betel nut. It was silly. They had just dropped their bags at the hotel. They should stick together. It's around the corner, Dad, come on.

No.

I'll be right back.

He had run off and been hit as Allison and Harry stood facing each other, cooly waiting for another of their flights to begin. They had to be prodded by the excited man who came running at them over the cobbles, hand on head, barefoot.

People had laid their bikes down at the end of the street.

"It's not a question of the betels, is it, of their being legal," Harry asked.

"Oh my God," Allison said. "Oh my God."

17

The house was in poor repair when they returned to Victoria's late summer. Harry went back to work. "You're not angry are you?" She muttered no. "I need something to do. There's a lot to do there," he had to say to her. Her tomatoes and herbs at the side of the house were scorched sticks, raw brown; with the rains they subsided to yellow and by October some limp green was swelling at them. Slowly the yard took on the rain. Harry had a lot of late work. The chimney was leaking a black rivulet that was working into a pool beneath the grate they had bought no wood for. She had dreams of raised platforms and flapping canvas, of mounds of turmeric and coriander whose edges dispersed over a cool tile floor a fragrance, a dalliance of particles, disturbing her. Far more than Harry's affair, for he was obviously having one.

Could ever.

The brightness of spice crushed on a floor, and signally lifting, it had a voice.

He thought at first they should try and go and have some fun, get out, so they did, to all the new bars in Victoria. They are about forty-five, Harry and Allison, so they go out, they still look youngish in jeans, but, as might be expected, the bars they have not been in for fifteen years are disconcerting to them. They drink too much. But at least it is interesting for Harry. He is ridiculously polite with the waitresses, he likes to have his coat hung up for him; she keeps hers on. It is cold in these places. There are ferns and girls and loud music. And a man on top of a woman, she thinks. Or the other way. Doing things. Is that it?

He thinks there will be another year of this, then they can re-establish, what has gotten into him.

She sees him carry his briefcase and umbrella over the lawn, get into the car and drive.

She goes always to the same corner, which has a history. It was where the bus dropped Mark off home from shops in junior high. It takes her about ten minutes. The area is younger. There's an elementary school, before her, and a rainy green tapestry: an alligator of kindergarteners with a young, slightly unstrung supervisor who stops them in their raincoats and boots. The children chatter happily and wait to cross the road. Everything laden. Green. And rained-on branches.The girl's eyes had turned to hers, found hers, in the rain before she could avoid them, and they were entirely empty of questions. Little girl in a hood. They had formed a bond not easily broken nor ever fully regained or recognizable to

18

her, then it was over, like a smell. Dank. Wild mint. The kinder-
garten line plashed away in rainbow plastics. Evening. A rind of
light on the road. She walked back home. It was a casual clarity,
nothing more, not grace.

There is a famous photograph of the Sikh tribes migrating after the
creation of Pakistan; the camera has created a frieze of the baggage,
the families, the eyes of the animals. The brushes they pass are of a
spiky, dense genus, fibrous and black, corralled out of the land.
They do not burn. They are firm, merged with their own shadows.
The few trees soar. Perhaps they were chosen by the photographer
as a sort of hominid accompaniment to tend the many legged,
many wheeled procession, which neither plods nor wavers.

    It is perfectly static, a caravan.

    In the Vedic period it was customary for the Indian tribes to
take songs with them when they journeyed into a new land. Each
new landscape was a new deity who demanded a new praise. The
travellers had to stop often and sing the verses in Pali, Telegu,
Sanskrit and these were the first recorded literatures of the
subcontinent.

    The Sikh photo is slightly overexposed. Men and women
appear faceless, yoked unencourageably to the oxen.

    How desperately inventive these chanted praises must have
been. How sincere. Certainly they were not alone. They would
have washed in new rivers and sang the verses they'd learned in
their own cities, then moved on. Over an ever-invented plain. The
brass shivers and a dwindling, insect drone of a drum banged.

My Father's Walks

My father walked everywhere. He never

drove. This is banal, as indeed a great deal about him was, but there was also the exceptional about this stern Englishman, prematurely bald with overreaching legs. He carried me near his centre on mornings in the nineteen-fifties as he struck out for work, myself in him, motion in motion, a tiny arrow in his quiver as his arms swung fairly before him. I had not meant to be so literary, but I can see it will take some doing.

Awkward, this: inflating what was to a recognizable shape, or the tendency to exaggerate, with me from an early age, my own arrows. Which of these I do not know. This I know: I am balding, my legs are too long, my facial bones are prominent. When I walk towards a destination I am not sure I will get there.

We lived then in Flemington Park, Toronto, a smaller concrete structure than the ranging apartments of Don Mills, which it neighbored, but large enough. There was a father, myself and a pregnant mother. One block was semi-circular and had eleven stories. From our balcony I could see all the way to the mall and road where it bent at the school to drop down, down past the stony brook and the decorative waterfall, steep into the ravine's reaching greenblack leaves— what elapsements of light therein, what a galaxy—and at the bottom the Don Mills expressway where the traffic of morning and evening flowed. Though hardly rich, we lived atop a lordly battlement; there was no part of Toronto I could not see.

In fact I could only see Scarborough, or Don Mills. One of the two.

I heard my father preparing to leave for work in the mornings; gather his macintosh and his brolly, lunchbag; then kiss my mother goodbye. I ran onto the balcony and waited. He came out six stories below, a set of head and shoulders, and strode across the street, making his usual shortcut across the triangular green behind the school. The brolly was rested on his shoulder. The lunch was tucked away in his pocket. Then his long legs could operate, and he stiffened and propelled, stiffened and propelled himself away, so small. The far corner of the school ate him up.

For a long time I thought that was where he worked and was heartened to learn that I would join him there when I was older.

My father had been in Canada for ten years, and he was not at home. He thought he was still in Salisbury, England, his

21

birthplace, in the nineteen-teens. But it was Toronto, 1963, Men wore homburgs and wonderful fedoras with dapper side-feathers, and baggy dark trousers. My mother had a pair of teardrop eyeglasses, just like Catwoman's, on TV. Cars were long and finned, soon to be boxy, and my father could not afford one. I watched him walk, every morning, until I could not see him any longer and felt even then that I did not understand the man. Why did he stiffen so? Why visibly flinch when a man in overalls carrying a metal pail greeted him? Or stop and never say a word to the one-legged man on a park bench, never greet him, but suddenly drop a coin in his cup and press on, faster, the old man waving, waving, and why did my father always walk alone? Quickly, distant, sun breaking through?

This is what I ask when I am tired or need the past.

The past, of course, does not need.

Which is its great attraction.

An illustration: I found out years later in a 1958 Toronto City Directory that my parents had lived elsewhere in that city, before my brother and I. I did not understand the listing, although I went over it many times and then looked through all the directories until the mid-sixties. This in Ottawa, the National Archives, well past midnight. I had been researching a feature article and the fluorescent lighting hummed, crackled. I wasn't tired, though I had been, and all sound dropped off as I read:

Sandcombe, Ronald S. (Elizabeth) 4753003
5-35678 Bristol A., Eng. lab. Ajax Carr.
8921213

From the key I learned that lab. was labourer; Ajax Carriage was a small shipping and loading firm in the Eglington district, which was poor, run down, and where one of the new subway stations were. But my parents did not marry until 1959.

Was the address a room in a boarding house or an apartment? Neither makes much sense. The solicitor of this information could have listed my mother in deference to my father's wishes. If it *were* a boarding house my mother would certainly not have lived with my father in it: women didn't. They took rooms with spinsters, then. Perhaps my father had recently secured their future apartment, and had given that new set of numbers, attempting to secure the place in print.

I got another coffee from the vending machine and forgot to press the button for extra sugar. The second listing I found went:

22

Sandcombe, Ronald S. (Betty E.M.) 4475910
603-1212 Harleybray D., Flem. Pk.
Tech. Wrtr. Philips Elec Scar. 7925001
(Jeffrey B. Mark W.)

I lost interest in the article I was supposed to be working on and rummaged through the directories until early morning. I found nothing more.

(Jeffrey B. Mark W.)

My brother and I thus entered the printed world. Today we are both writers. He is a poet and I am a novelist. It is, after all, a small alphabet. (Might Directories, Inc., later changed their policy and did not list children until they had attained the age of majority; it was thought that such data was superfluous, of interest only to pederasts. So future questers were to fall short of this fortune of finding themselves suddenly *entered*; before they had been nought, merely potentialities at the nexus of man, woman and property, a residence on early earth, listed in the red, thick-bound books in the predawn heart of another city.) I compared the two listings. Five years, two children, a change of place and occupation, both slightly upwards: technical writer, Philips Electronics.

He took us there once, by bus. It was a white and bright metal building, a low plant surrounded by expressways in Don Mills. There were record pressing factories nearby. No trees. It was a Saturday and we had gone to his office to pick up a few papers. My baby brother was in his arms and I walked. I sat in a plastic orange chair in the cafeteria and drank Coke while I waited. He finally appeared in the doorway burdened by my brother, his briefcase, and a few paperback books.

In 1965 our family moved to Winnipeg because he lost his job and my mother's parents were generous about it and took us in. I thought about that and gathered up my things to leave the archives. Then I did this: I took the two directories and hid them beneath a pile of almanacs and walked quickly out onto Rideau Street. It was early and there was no traffic so I walked down the middle of the road with my coat open and watched the sun stream in the vast glass mirror of the Bank of Canada building. Then I walked home. Under the Queensway. Past the frozen canal and past the empty stadium. Among the people who would later fill those tiers of seats, who would walk that sidewalk, a little later in the day.

Sandcombe, Ronald S. Before Elizabeth, E.M. and Mark and Jeffrey, where was he?

23

I know now that he was in Northern Ontario and Northern Quebec. He knew about radios, about tubes and codes, Morse and otherwise; he knew these things from the war. Doubtless they helped him become a technical writer, but they don't help me very much. There existed a tallish man, a veteran of some sort, uninjured, who had difficulty talking to others and who must have arrived here by boat, in Montreal, sometime in the early fifties or late forties. He would have smoked Senior Services in Britain and switched to Players in Canada; then quit. North, among those dorsal and saurian rocks, that waste of wind and snow, he must have been cold and bitter and, for a time, very much alone.

I wonder. He never talked about his family.

They were either dead or in Australia, it seemed.

It seemed also that he was older than he was.

Married older, was old with children.

Stiff.

I have never been to Salisbury; perhaps I should go. It is near Stonehenge, another code, another press of rocks. I asked my father once about that place.

"Why would you ask Jeffrey? Why on earth would you want to know?"

I didn't answer. He placed his hands on his knees and looked sideways at my mother, who encouraged him to continue.

"I have nothing to say about that time or that place," he said.

"He is only curious," my mother put in.

Still he would not speak. He returned to reading *The Ipcress File* which was later made into a black and white movie he took me to see when I was seven. I didn't understand it. The action involved a train, a briefcase and Berlin. Maybe not Berlin. Maybe London and Berlin was *The Spy Who Came in from the Cold* starring Richard Burton and Tuesday Weld. All irrelevant.

"Betty," he said, "I think some tea would be nice."

By this time I had returned to my bedroom.

"He talks to you, your son talks to you and you tell him nothing. What do you think, he isn't old enough to talk? He talks all day, why and how and what, and I respond."

Their voices were pure, at a new level, exasperated, patient.

"He has not been there and myself, I have not been there for a long time. I cannot see the use of it. There are more suitable subjects to discuss and you may tell him that."

"You may fix your own tea, then."

I can hear them, parental, hovering near anger on that grey afternoon with my brother near me and starting to make noises with his tongue against the two filthy windowpanes and the towering language of distant apartment blocks.

When I was twenty-seven I wrote a poem about my father leaving Salisbury, which I have always seen as a sepia and barren place.

> Flatness, flatness and a calm
> And calm's interior regret at no
> Uphill or agitation, no strain still
> Against a pressure, pull. The land extends....

Then there was some crap about the rivers fingers of an indolent hand and mist around the here and there black trees and, worse, my ancestors "...more visible to others, held / In bones around my eyes." The poem concluded:

> The family house was stone, had held
> The delicacy of curtains to the light.
> He walked to the train-platform, and heard
> The low throat of his going some ways off.
> He looked back,
> > And was gone.
> > > Since you asked
> About the past, I'd say to know
> This little is desire itself, will do.
> What else is home?

I do not like it. I liked it once because it had, for me, a certain noble resignation. In my worst moments I thought it Audenesque. But it is smug and sententious and it is not enough.

Here are a few of my father's walks.

The first occurred when we were still in Toronto. There are many; he was on a lifelong constitutional; but this one stood out, exception, or miracle. He was a Rosicrucian and an avid reader of paranormal paperbacks. I doubt there existed a phenomena in which he did *not* believe; this was a condition of his innerness, his slight estrangement from his peers. He had colleagues in the Order, but not friends. They and he were coevally contiguous at the Hall, with its purple baize and golden roping, the prepossessing altar around which they joined hands; but they never came to our apartment and my father never went anywhere, save work, without my mother.

It was like this: he told my mother and I overheard. So did my brother, an even more curious individual than myself. We were in the hall closet, eavesdropping on my mother's frequent conversations with the supper ingredients, when we heard, in rapid slip-slap, his steps and his entrance. It was Saturday and he had been at the Rosicrucian Hall all afternoon.

"It's happened," he said.

"Sit down, and tell me. What was it?"

"Dear, I had but exited from the Hall and was walking to the bus stop when I felt weak, very under it, you know.... Is there something hot to drink?"

"Sit down, I'll make it."

My brother whispered "cocoa" in my ear, which he often did, but I gagged him.

"I want to say that I love you Betty."

"I love you too, Ron. Now. You were at the bus stop, and..."

"I did not attain the bus stop. As I was relating, I felt ill and stopped and closed my eyes. Betty, I do not know what happened. When I opened them I was at Philips."

I felt the indraw of my brother's breath on my hand-skin.

"Let me feel your forehead, Ron."

"No, no. I was at Philips. I know I was because I leaned against the wall outside——surely you know it, white wall——the long, white wall. And I saw the Philips' sign."

"Quite sure you're all right? No, sit."

"I'm fine. I was at Philips. Then I was outside the tobacconist's, not five hundred yards from here."

"Yes, you got here rather quickly."

"I think I'm developing it, the ability."

"Be quiet," my mother said, "be very quiet. Lie down. Here, I've made you this to drink."

"Betty? Something stronger? That good rye? I've changed my mind. I have a very strong feeling, Betty, that I'm gifted in some way; I can do things with my mind."

"Yes, of course, now lie down, please, I'll tend to the boys."

Later, when we crept out of the closet, he was sleeping. In the corner of the couch, his drink untouched. One lamp was on, limning his skull-skin. My mother herded us into the kitchen for soup and touched her fingers to her lips: "Your father is resting."

I don't doubt he had to. After the walk; also after having told my mother so seriously that he loved her: that had never happened before within earshot. The worst thing was, for me, the way that he had said he was gifted, with too much stress on the word, as if he had been dying to say it someday; he'd always known it and was then on the threshold of a deeper deception, something terrible and cozening and frightening to know or hear or speak of in the light of day.

He liked to tell me that if you looked at yourself in a mirror in a darkened room by the light of a single candle you would see your appearance in a past life.

Many years after I understood that these things he said were not necessarily lies, untruths, that he might have, blink, contracted time and space that afternoon; he may well have been telekinetic. But I will have to explain a little.

It was at Grand Beach, Manitoba; I was ten, my brother seven. We had gone for a week to stay in a motel, a small vacation. It was a hot summer and the water fine for swimming. My mother took off her headscarf on the beach and served us sandwiches, and my father wore Bermuda shorts. We could see the thin, far shore of the lake and the waving wet grasses of the lagoon to the south. There was an aluminum shack near the lagoon where a man with a silver tooth sold perch and catfish wrapped in yellowed Tribunes; around him was a curtsey-ring of weeping willows.

Father meditated all week. Meditated and channelled.

My mother spread the grey blanket and fixed the wind-breaker umbrella; she readied the tape recorder and switched it on. Father's face grew even older, took on a warm shock as he began to speak in a voice different from his own. My mother fussed over the tapes and with the microphone as he droned. We the children built sandcastles and crushed them. The afternoons and channellings were very long and we were hungry when he stopped; but we all had to sit still for a while, in a circle, and not move quickly, not speak, while he recovered, stirred. Four of us black against the sand and water. The sun set orange and mauve. We packed up and returned to the hotel for soup and eggs.

"It's not a vacation for me if I have to cook all the time," said Mother.

The subjects of Father's channellings varied. They had to do with spiritual energies. They had to do with negative vibrations. They mentioned the aethereal and astral planes. And they were delivered through him by personages with comic-book names:

Yolanda, Sananda, Mark-El, Char-Koo. It was comforting to know that my father was important to these beings; otherwise, how would they speak? How would they tell us that:

The earth was surrounded by veils, seven of them, that separated the channel from his correspondents.

There was work to be done, tremendous work to be done.

Richard Nixon was a carrier of light-energy, a very old soul.

Pierre Trudeau was, on the other had, extremely un-aethereal. There was some hope for his wife.

Chakras and kundalinis existed. Mu and Atlantis were.

And all of us had astral bodies which were silver and radiant and extremely light.

"Where's mine?"

"Having cocoa, shut up."

We learned from Lord El-Ray on the afternoon before we returned to Winnipeg that many many years ago the whole area, the Interlake, had been covered by water; it was therefore "a very spiritual place" and had "great energies". He spoke of Lake Aggasiz and the Manitou as if reading from a coffee-table book, through my father, through his eyes and working mouth, and finished his communique with a sonorous chant.

OOOOOOOOOOOOOOOOOOMMMMMMMMMMMMMMMM.

A wind came upon us, chilly; I was afraid and clung to my father's hand as we passed the granite boulders on the way to our room. I could not keep up to his stride and he rebuked me. I yelled at him. We stood against each other in the middle of the road. A line of pelicans, white, slow and majestic, flapped far above us beneath a grey-fringed cloud.

And I began to remember water, cold, deep water. I took his hand again and we walked on, he at a more moderate pace, and I began to forget.

The next morning we had our bags at the roadside well before the Grey Goose bus arrived.

The motel owner waddled up to my father and hoped that his stay had been pleasant. Ed Nemeth, he was.

"Ronald Sandcombe." He shook Mr. Nemeth's hand diplomatically, at full length.

My mother and brother were watching frogs leap about near the ditchpump; trailing bright waterdrops; and I was five years old again, in the spring, and there was a pool with a deep end near our apartment block and I walked around, warm, happy, because the grey frazels of ice partly covered the dirty water and shone and flimsily gaped open in places.

"So, did you enjoy the beach?" Mr. Nemeth said.

"Indeed. In my time I have been to Brazil and visited the finest beaches in the world and the beach you have here is their equal. I believe we shall return."

"That's nice," said Nemeth. "Brazil, eh?"

"That was a while ago, longer than I care to remember."

"That's in Europe, right?"

"The South Americas, actually."

There was a moment when I was right up to the water and saw the slick and greeny twigs slant towards it and then a next when a twig touched my cheek and the cold and I was in it, thrashing, turning in a panic around and around to see the steep sloped cement and the godly buildings beyond the edge and I gasped, reached for the ladder and slipped and swallowed a lot of water, and reached, again, slipped back, deep into the cold and I was tired and crying——I cried and cried——and I stood beside the pool and breathed, and breathing saw the gashes in the ice, each breath, and was I in or out of the water, the murder, the grip of the water and ran, I ran to the apartment and yelled and yelled at my mother; but how did I get out of it?; and I knew. Philips Electronics.

"Oh, yeah, like Mexico," said Mr. Nemeth.

I very quietly went and picked up my duffel bag and stood still by the road.

"Kid going somewhere?" said Nemeth.

"He's a very independent sort," said Father.

"Yeah, I see that."

Thus I am also a believer, albeit a minor and frightened one.

When we got on the bus I saw Mr. Nemeth take off his cap and wave it at me, once. We started to move. I grabbed my father's arm because I thought he should wave back, but he would not; I could tell he had been angered by their little chat. When I looked back that little man was gone.

Understand that I do not approve of my father's rudeness. Or of channelling. Or of astral bodies or negative vibrations or spiritual energies.

There are no veils about this world but the ones we see when we close our eyes, tight, clench them, and we imagine death, those retinal webs, those corridors.

No easy journeys.

There are instead rescues and martyrdoms and, for a time, the situation of one elderly man collecting the unearthly desires of the young around him, the bearded and sandalled and credulous, those for whom religion must seem a better parent with gaudier gifts, a ferris wheel, all the cumbersome machinery of circuses. They sat around my father lotus style and he raised his face and spoke the words of others in the dim light; they were grateful, as after a decent concert, but they did not like him. Though I never believed in his powers that way, not through worship, they were not unlike me. They exchanged recipes for fenugreek tea and wheatgerm cookies with my mother and discussed healing in a condescending way with him when the channellings had finished for the evening. And the women breast fed their babies, named "Sky" or "Cloud" in front of myself and my brother; I felt desire; my father never noticed, too deep in his spell.

One or two things happened, yes. Apparently. But I am not so gifted to regard them as my heritage, the truth of self.

I have said that I do not approve, yet there is in me an iota of belief that will not die, as perhaps it should. Because of the pool, the drowning, and the voices that sounded of slow metal wings in my father's mind: all the sick evidence of his transcendence. Labourer, technical writer, amateur adept. Angel of the world's most visited beaches, angel of my near burial in snow.

One Winnipeg February I was at a friend's place. We were casually destroying a cardboard service station and pocketing the miniature cars, when I was called to the phone. My father's voice was angry in my ear.

"Your mother doesn't know where you are."

"Well, I'm at Bobby's, obviously."

"She's worried sick. Get home now."

I bundled up and set out. It was very cold. I made fists in my mitts to keep my hands warm and walked sideways past the big school near Assiniboine Park, then turned into the park. Snow whipped off the crust and flew in a powder in the air, and it was getting dark, so I decided to cut across the field between the pavilions and the river-bridge. At the bridge I could slow down. Home was just across it and a block. A boy made compact and barely visible in my tawny parka, I clambered over a bank of ice and snowboulders and ran with some glee into the field, where the wind met me furiously. It was not too bad and I trudged on. I saw the slow mass of the winter river far away and the lights of the cars beyond the bridge, the way they threw cones that stopped, blunt, in the twilight. It began to snow. My foot plunged through the crust, I worked it out. Then the other. Plunge, struggle, another step, down I went again.

I stood to my knees in snow and saw the beautiful shape of the wind and the flakes on the orange-blue surface and licked my lips, cracked, chapped, continued on.

Ten minutes later I had gone fifty yards or less. My shin got barked on something and I cried out; the wind shrieked. Ahead was the pavilion, its turreted shape. The object was a frozen-together cricket-wicket. It jutted through the crust.

My pants were stiff, wet. My feet hurt.

I lay on my side to rest. The snow, there was so much of it, flew level across the field and gusted at my face, stung my eyes. I was tired. There, I would rest a little and then go home. When I turned my head there were the lamps on the distant bridge, a rounded line of lambencies, and the snow filing ever down in the far darkness. In my father's TIME-LIFE GREAT RELIGIONS OF THE WORLD book I had read that Mahomet the Prophet had toppled a cup and, in that instant, flew all across Arabia to Jerusalem on his white horse then caught the cup, the cup of milk. I wished for it.

My lashes, my lashes.

And it came.

It whirled at me in a blast of breath and crystal.

It slung me over it reeling.

It carried me over the bridge to the warmth, to the lights, to the hall outside our apartment.

And it smoothed my hair, set me on my feet, and said, "Tell your mother nothing of this."

What could I tell my mother for what did I know? How had he found me?

It is certainly not because of his later breakdown when he couldn't channel and he sat alone in his study and read *A Dweller on Two Planets* by Phylos and *The Sacred Symbols of MU* by Churchward and everything by Erich von Daniken. Our house was empty again in the evenings and the interested people, decades his juniors, stopped dropping by. He became angry and stayed angry. He forbade my brother and I to listen to rock music, wear jeans, or go out with our friends. These are the usual intolerances of the old, but he displayed them without perspective, became pitiful, nasty, unlovely to be with or behold.

31

He raged and cried.

At the unions and at the New Democrats.

At the workers at the job he'd gotten by walking from door to door for three months in 1965. They were "Only to labour by the sweat of their brows, my son, like filthy animals, yea, the sweat of their brows!"

And I turned from him in disgust, couldn't save him, didn't want to. He turned from me. He subscribed to *Mark Age Publications, The Journal of Extraterrestrial Research,* and the *National Enquirer.*

Veins broke in his forehead and marked him.

He destroyed my records and my cassettes; he took away my paper route; he told my brother and I that, had he gone to our schools, he would have graduated *summa cum laude.* He shook his fist.

"SUMMA CUM LAUDE!" Smashed his hand on the cadenza.

There are no words of my mother, spoken in front of her sons, to record. (Elizabeth.) My father was again alone. His nose quivered. He tried to channel again, repeatedly, but it was no good, the gift was gone and the messages were tight in him now, coiled, explosive.

He threw me out of the house when I turned fifteen.

"I have no love left in my heart for you," he said.

I didn't believe him. I believed him later. I don't believe him.

"Can you believe it?" people often say.

The stupid fools: not much later, in the family court, he disowned me, using the words "guttersnipe" and "miserable, worthless tramp".

The last calm exchange I had with him occurred more than a dozen years ago. It is all too clear. He was interested in the Bermuda Triangle that year, read voluminously on the subject. Near suppertime one day I went to our window and saw his usual bus pull up a kilometre away at the hockey arena. My father, small yet undeniably he, got off, and began his walk towards our house, skirting the football field, marching along beside the row of duplexes. It was a brisk fall day; clouds scudded and the sound of firecrackers rang from the neighboring streets. Everything was green but deep, as in slumber or dream, beginning to toss in colour and to turn. He walked toward me with his raincoat, his umbrella, but he could not see me. His hem flapped. He held onto

32

his fedora tightly. I wanted to welcome him so I met him at the door.

"Hello, Dad," I said, "how was work?"

He looked surprised, then darkened.

"Can't you think of something better to ask me?" he said.

"Sure." This was quite unconscious; I was trying hard to interest him. "Why the Bermuda Triangle? I mean why do you read so much about it?"

He looked me up and down.

Set his hat on the end table.

"My brother died in an airplane crash there before the war. Excuse me."

And he went to put away his lunchpail and be with my mother, like any labourer at the end of the work-day.

I will not likely see him again; but I feel, now and then, that he sees me, as clearly as the sky or a change in weather.

I wish I could see him on a March afternoon in 1960, on the loading dock at Ajax Carriage. Yes. He leans on a forklift and nods at the men who, passing him, slap him on the back, roughhouse him. He smiles. He acknowledges their cheer. But he waits until the place is silent, empty of all men, before he sits with his hands clasped around his knees and smiles to himself. The wind catches a loose newspaper, which skids past him, flaps, and sails on. He rehearses his wife's earlier phone call. He thinks of how lightly and quickly the afternoon went. It is almost dark outside; the lights and the noise subdued; the factories shut down. He gathers his few things and shrugs his jacket on, thinks of picking up a bouquet of blossoms, carnations, on their way home. No chrysanthemums. And he begins to walk, happy, quite confident that the child will be a son.

Tapirance

The hour was when supper was set in

the little girl's neighborhood. The lawns were serenely in touch with the houses and curbs and the blue-white street lamps on. Inside the large windows of the homes furniture was seen, tall, polished and dark, hulking over the people who were smoothing tablecloths, placing tureens gently down, adjusting plates with their palms.

Many of the houses had chimes, or music boxes attached to the doorbells. With luck these would ring out when the door was opened, or in the middle of love. It was also pleasant to hear them, and hear them again tinily in the evening when the best breezes were.

The little girl —Penny-June—sat, insolent, with her parents at the table. Her arms were heavy and fisted around the plate of food she would not touch. She would not touch it for a thousand years, if necessary. Let them suffer

She listened to her parents chew and swallow and juice their mouths with water.

Not too disgusting, she thought. Like the petting zoo, get out.

Her father, Mr. Andrews, held up a drumstick and proclaimed: "Great, Hon. It's not your regular turkey."

"Gravy?"

"Please."

Mr. Andrews wore a tie at dinner; Mrs. Andrews a dress. What were they up to? It was diabolical; they looked like her, but why were they so strange? Why did her father put his pipe on the breadplate that way?

"Hard day, dear?" she, with a single pearl on, said.

"I worked like a dog. Big order."

"A nice bonus this year would be nice."

Any minute, just wait, they're going to fold their hands and smile sweetly at me. Then they're either going to ask me about school or tell me that I'm adopted. And... "Yes, Father?"

"The salt. Could you please."

"Sure. Why not more gravy? Have some, Daaad, get faaaat."

"Penny-June!" went Mother, barely audible, chin at a tautness.

"That's my name," said Penny and got up, and marched to her room. She slammed the door.

"Yes, go to your room," she heard the boom of her father's

words. Then silence, broken a little later by sobbing, and a few whispers out there in the house, neither of which concerned Penny, cross-legged on her canopied bed, staring at her posters. They were wow to her; she liked to look at the golden friendly boys and pretend she was married to each of them. She said her new names over and over again in the nightlighted room and looked out the bay window at the branches of the oak. Penny Phoenix—so beautiful. Arm in arm with him, River. Mrs. Michael J. Fox, Penelope Fox. No way they'd believe her, no way.

Penny June Jackson? Totally rad.

She curled up and she went to sleep and she had a curious dream. The room was nightlighted and very dark and Penny saw a tiny pig—its paws, no, its hooves—held up, that turned out of the small dark corner and walked upright, prancing almost, towards her, larger, a large pig, impressive.

Penny's head drifted up from her pillow. The sleek pig was smiling at her. The pig at the foot of the bed wore a diamond-patterned housecoat and a bathing cap.

"Excuse me," it said.

A girl, thought Penny.

"Excuse me, but I was told you have chocolate." The pig, whoever it was, was a little too friendly when she said 'chocolate', a little slimy, and Penny began to look around the room for some means of escape or explanation. Her years of TV-watching told her what to look for; there were no signs of a forced entry.

"I'm terribly sorry to have wakened you," the animal continued, "but it was a matter of chocolate and, well, you understand."

Then Penny woke up.

"Well, where is it, my dear?"

"Under the bed."

Penny rolled and was off the bed and the pig sought her, rolled her back, pinned her down.

"A little frisky, are we? I'm Miss Tapir."

"T-tapir."

"Peggy Tapir to you."

"I'm P-penny June."

"My what a lovely name. Where's the chocolate, Juney Penney?"

"My shoulders hurt and anyway besides I can't move them you're on me." She paused. It might not be a good idea to call Miss Tapir fat, not at this stage. "Please let me move and I'll give you all

36

the chocolate you want."

"That I doubt," the pig said.

But she got off and Penny went and opened her cupboard and brought out a box of Black Magic.

"They're all I've got," she said as she handed it over, her nightie huge around her ankles.

"Shut up. Open it."

There was an interval of eating. The pig and Penny slowly ate the whole box, arguing over the creams and tossing the fruit-gums out the window. Then they took turns with the walnuts and almonds. Sighing, they finished, and Miss Tapir closed the box.

"That," she said, "was fingersucking *yum*."

"Was it?" said Penny. Somehow she had only gotten five chocolates, even with all the protocol that the pig had insisted on.

"I believe it was, yes."

They grinned.

"Have you more, my dear?"

"Baclava?" Penny said slyly.

"Come again," said the pig.

"Sticky? Pistachio rich? Honey-humming and puffy from the pan?"

"*Indeed*."

"I don't have baclava."

Miss Tapir darkened. Her bathing cap hovered at her ears. "Nasty," she said, "Nasty that's all you are, bony sickthing stick of a vicious little girl."

"More chocolate, then?"

"And I'm not speaking to you."

"Raisin bars."

"Be quiet."

She hammed a swoon and sweetly said, "*L'eclair ultime*."

"Child..."

"Whipped cream I would think like a cloud so like it can be cinnamon sprinkled?"

"Where? Where?"

"I don't have the foggiest."

This time the tapir laughed and scampered over the sheets, and back. "May you waste away," she said, "please."

The door to the dark room opened, a square tower of light with Father in it.

"Penny? Penny?" went Mr. Andrews.

His hand was on the knob. The pig was cowering behind

Penny, trembling, gripping her at the hips. "Is it a p-panther," she whispered.

"What panther?" said Mr. Andrews. "Penny, why that's preposterous."

"Daddy? Did I say panther? Oh, Daddy, I must have been dreaming."

"Then you should dream quietly, Penny, for the sake of your mother."

"Is she asleep?"

"Wrapped up in Carson," said Mr. Andrews, and with a quick look around the room, shut the door.

Penny turned to comfort the pig who was breathing very very fast, and this made her hard to comfort. For instance Miss Tapir carried on like this for a bit, like.

"Dear me Ah dear Ah me. Ah. A panther, th. Ah, ahh ahh ahh. No reason, no reason to be scared now. And Ah. And Ahh. No fear. No panther. P-panther," she went.

"There is no panther," she said firmly and finally and adjusted her bathing cap. "I must be off nevertheless."

"So soon?"

"Yes, and thank you for the chocolate."

Miss Tapir gathered her housecoat up, tucked in her tail, and with a wave and a See You, walked backwards in a clever curve, and turned into the corner, and was smaller and gone.

Come morning, the blue jays and sparrows were upset in the oak and the leaves were very clear on her wall and Penny was tired and hungry. She listened carefully for parental hum and there was none; she padded lightly to the pantry. No one seemed present. Her hand was on one of the finer marmalades and lifting it silently down.

"Penny-June!"

"Mother!"

Smash. Mess. Glass.

"Oh, Penny, you will hurt yourself, I swear. Out of that mess."

"Yes, Mother."

She slunk into the backyard and watched her father negotiate a mangling of the lawnmower cord. A croquet peg and a baseball bat and a small lawnchair had become involved, while the lawnmower stood there, freshly primed and impatient. Father produced a pipe, and kicked up a little leafstorm as he puffed, circling the mower with an eye to solutions and the nefarious yardthings in his way. He looked like a nervous sportscaster.

Like no way he's my father.

Presently Mother came out and handed her a cheese sandwich.

"Cheese: bleck. Milk: double bleck."

"It's all you're getting."

"Good."

"Penny...."

"Look, just don't gross me out Mom. Okay?"

Much later in the afternoon Penny wandered into the basement den where Father was tuned in with alacrity to the football game. He rooted for Dallas—"America's Team," he said to her without looking up, and she nodded. "That Landry is a fine coach. The best!" Penny tolerated the game: the men tried over and over to *heave* this ball into a *crowd*—why?—; and the dances at half-time were okay. But after father grew dark in the third quarter, and Mother popped in to say she was off to shop, Father grew darker as Dallas began to lose it. When they conceded a safety touch, down by seven, he switched the channel.

Alarming.

In a sunset scenario a moustachioed dwarf stood, waves breaking at his chest. Native dancers materialized behind him; nasal music; he began to speak. "Hello. This is Horst Kohler and today I am with you *in the* Island paraDise of *Ha-vie-ee.*"

Alarming. Father likes it.

Coconuts on Bermuda shorts.

Hawaii, get away.

Still, he likes it...

Halfway through the program he got onto the whetstone and started working on the carving knife. Penny was so bored she got interested in the couch-cushions and then she saw the chocolate.

It was in a pink sateen box with a curlicular ribbon and it was between the Bowling Kiwanis trophy and the curling Heather Club medallion—both Father's.

"Daddy," she said.

"Child?"

"When did you win those?"

"Silly, you don't win cigarettes. Prefer the pipe but I keep these on hand. For the Rose Bowl."

"Oh.

"Daddy?"

"Yes, muffin."

"I mean the shiny trophies up there?"

"Oh those. Those were a while ago. Quite a while."

"Daddy can I touch them?"

"Be careful."

On closer inspection the chocolate box proved to be pleasingly hefty when she budged it from the shelf. But for the time she let it rest there. It had begun, she knew it. It was like too much. She had seen the sharp the carving knife and now it was a question merely of her flight, and her abandonment, and before she was an orphan again how much she could steal from her *parents*—she practically spit it out—who would be terrified as this girl fled from village to village. Wading the rivers, living on fruits. But she would work up to all that, beginning with the chocolate box.

Then Father packed away the carving knife and Penny smelt Yorkshire pudding all light and yellow in a pan and Father walked up the stairs with his legs and she heard the unctual buzzing, like a violent fly, of the electric knife.

Dinner was over soon and it was night.

Mother and Father went to bed early, between towers of paperbacks and damp towels. She heard their first snores.

Miss Tapir was waiting for her in the rhubarb. The leaves cleared, and Miss Tapir greeted her: "Please come in."

"It's dark."

"I know. Please enter."

"It's *dark*," Penny said again with pressure on the *d*, with meaning.

"What?"

"The chocolate."

Miss Tapir stepped out of the rhubarb rather quickly. "Why didn't you say so, child? We must have a plan. Where is it?"

"The den."

"The den."

There was a pause.

"Not a panther den?"

"Father's den."

"Cheers, then. We do the den and the dirty deed and dine on chocolate. Agreed?"

"Greed," said Penny-June.

They made their way around the back of the home tiptoeing through the garden. "Horrid things," Miss Tapir snorted.

"Vegetables."

Then they were clutching their hands and doing knee bends near the trellis. They saw downrunning ivy and the rung of the eavestrough far above. Then they rooted around the building. "No window," Miss Tapir finally said.

"None."

"Molish person your father, no?"

"Creep."

"How much chocolate is there?"

"Quite a large amount I should think," said Penny.

"Right. There's a chimney. Up we go. There is a chimney?"

"I think so. Yes, there is."

"Up we go."

But before she did anything she took out a stocking and worked its shadow over her head. She had some trouble with her snout.

She swung a clove up and said, "Tapirance!"

Penny didn't get it and didn't care. In minutes they were halfway up the trellis and eating their share of ivy leaves by accident. When she was scared she clung to Miss Tapir's tail; when she wasn't she rested and pointed out places to the pig, for the moon was up and she saw all the way down George Street to the Edward Smith skating rink which was a silver oval through the tree branches; but she didn't dare dawdle; the pig was unusually persuasive and indeed determined to achieve the eavestrough, which was level and, with a huff and a puff and a push from Penny, held. They lay on the roof and went "Whew!"

Then they crept to the slanted housing of the brick chimney and put their heads together. Somewhere in the neighborhood of the Hawkins' a dog barked.

The home was not silent.

Upstairs: Mr. Wilson stirred and groped for his flashlight. He saw that his wife was asleep and roused himself, nervous. Was somebody upstairs or downstairs? he wondered.

He slipped into his kimono and stood in the hallway, the landing, his hand on the bannister, in the cool kitchen.

Downstairs, he decided. He got hold of a flyswatter and gripped it and the flashlight and a tennis racket. He had trouble locating the lightswitch, and even more trouble switching it; but he trod very quietly down to his den.

The girl and the pig were balled up together in the chimney, scratching their way downwards. Miss Tapir had gone

41

first, and Penny could have told her that this wasn't sensible at all Penny had to push and cajole the pig every few seconds. Frankly, she thought, this was turning into a lot of trouble, perhaps more than the hefty box of chocolate warranted. But it seemed injudicious to back out now; if the pig stuck upwards there'd be no way to push her. And Miss Tapir, though struggling, was optimistic.

"Not far now," she muttered. "A little chocolate in store for us, yum. We could have used a hippo for this. The hippo is a summer sort of fellow, not to say lazy, but a master of plans. He is especially sagacious if sweets are the issue. So a hippo would have helped. But I see a light down there, a tiny light..."

"There," went Father. "That ought to make it toastier."

And he ripped A-J from the phone book and lay the pages on a swivelling, finicky flame.

The pages caught.

"Do you smell something?" said Miss Tapir.

"No. Yes."

"Is it smoke?"

"It is."

"Geronimo!" squealed Miss Tapir and scrabbled harder downward.

Father was a little dozy and sat in his chair, pointed directly at the ashes that came batting out of the fireplace and fell lightly about his bare knees.

"Push, child, *push!*" said the pig.

"Now what was that?" Mother sat straight up in bed and gasped. Where was her husband? She swept her sheets around her and raced into Penny's room where she saw it: the bed empty and the curtains whipping out the window. For the wind was up and as she flew down the stairs a singeing scent met her. A fire! A fire! Into the kitchen she filled a huge pail with soapy water she dipped up. A good deal of this soaked her legs and the sheet when she started down the stairs.

Thus there were three things falling very fast when Father woke up. He'd been admiring the flouncing curves of the flaming pages as they crawled into ash, quite asleep, when *bang*, when *bsssshash* when *babababadder shhh* he awakened.

He saw his wife behind him.

The pig yelped in the ashes.

His wife got up, she advanced, she swung a pail, and let go, and water washed the fireplace in a hissing splash.

42

Penny-June plopped in a grey puddle near the pig.

His wife, in a wet sheet, blubbered at his feet, and the pig shot far under the couch, dragging Penny-June.

"I-I-is it out?" his wife said.

"The pig or the fire?" he said.

"Fire."

"It's out, honey. Get up, please."

"And the pig?"

"Can't see it."

"And Penny?"

"Disappeared."

And the wind got down the chimney and the mist of ashes in the den's air in layers settled on them as they slept. The girl and the pig, holding hands, reached up for the chocolate and exited, pretty pleased with themselves. Miaow, went the Ferguson's cat, miaow in the windy backlane, in the garbage can.

In the morning things got tidied up early and Mother and Father had a dilatory breakfast in the kitchen. Penny was nowhere to be seen.

Around eleven Mother went up to her room. The door was locked.

Around noon she went again. The door opened.

Penny was kicking her foot, feet, on the bed and propped on her elbows eating chocolate.

"Hello, dear. Good morning," Mother said.

"Is Father mad?"

"He hasn't mentioned it."

"I hate him."

"Well..."

Penny offered her mother a chocolate and kneeled beside her, questioningly.

"He's not going to ground me?"

"Child, it was his phone book. And though I don't have the foggiest what you—you and that pig were doing in the fireplace, I'm sure it's forgiven. The home didn't burn down and that's all I ask."

Penny was silent.

"Where did the pig go?" said Mother.

"She went back to her riverbank."

"I see..."

"Tapirs—not pigs, tapirs live on riverbanks," said Penny. "This is in Africa. They live on riverbanks and are quite afraid of their only enemy, the panther. Which my friend, I'm afraid to say, thought Father was."

"Your father a panther? Preposterous"

"Not to a tapir. Anyways she's gone like my only friend."

The two women sat with their feet tucked under them on the pink bedspread. After a while they could hear Mr. Wilson, conscious now, calling their names, not unfurtively.

"It's not like I've got a million friends like," said Penny.

"You've got me here."

Penny looked at her. Well, maybe she was. And maybe she wasn't.

"Do you want that hot chocolate, Penny? I've been thinking. I should start treating you, well, a little different."

"What do you mean?"

"I mean you're a big girl, a young woman almost."

Penny considered it.

"A young tapir," she said, firmly.

"All right, my dear. A young tapir."

"Shall we go to see what the panther wants?" said Penny-June. "He sounds like anxious."

Sweet Embroidery

Every summer the Northern Telecom

plant shut down for two weeks and for two weeks the community halls and beer parlours of Belleville would be full. Men would wear white, short-sleeved shirts around the raised dance floor at Gatsby's, or would luminously circle the blacklighted stage at the Canadian, sweating.

Now they shut off their machines, and wiped these with cloths, and walked in a long, tidy line to the Main Floor Time Punch. Already a chatter was rising from them.

"So, what you going to do, Joe?"

"Nothing."

"For two weeks?"

"You bet."

Joe was at the end of the line, impatient. He had a bowling tourney in Kingston in an hour, televised. His daughter would watch him tomorrow, after her cartoons.

He punched out and walked to his Chrysler.

It was slow, hot, getting through the parking lot. Groups strayed into his driving, holding beer bottles, shouts of hello. He smiled and drove at a prowl through them. Gliding along the back road, gliding past the company tennis courts, he made the Wooler Road turn in a light dust and rode up that cloud, and shifted to neutral coming down so the Moira Road rose to meet him, and the yellow, northern cornfields, his hometown——he worked the ruts, bumps and gravel wash of the crooked lane and the tiny house he pulled up at.

Joe kicked his tire and looked up that lane: his father-in-law's garden looked good, a lot better than that dead man did, and a helluva lot better than his brother-in-law's black Buick. Curtains shot back. The old woman's nose was mashed, for a second, against the pane and she waved, quite tiny; it took Joe aback. He entered his own house.

"I'm home."

A powder-blue bed took up the whole kitchen.

"About time you showed, Joe. This good man's come to sell us a bed."

The salesman's hat was off, his hand came out, Joe shook it, once. The man shrugged, looked away. He plainly suffered from the heat.

And his wife's voice went: "The bed tilts for your bad back, Joe, look."

"A real beauty," said the salesman.

"I don't want a bed. Where's my daughter?"

His wife shot up. How strange her face was to him! The salesman bent to examine a doily. "Now that is some sweet embroidery," he muttered; and the bed, with a sudden hum, began to tilt.

The little girl woke up beside Joe outside Gananoque. She rubbed the sleep from her eyes and said, "Daddy? Will I still see you on TV?"

"Christ, I hope not," he said, thinking of police, the news. But he thought on it a spell, and presently whispered at her, "*You won't have to.*" And he drove on. "You're gonna be there, muffin. On *television.*" And he drove on.

The Girl Who Met Goethe

Once upon a time, in a faraway village

by a tricky river near a large, dark forest your mother was young. Today she is old, and deserves her rest. (And that is why you are with me.) In the days I'll tell you of she was beautiful, and got little. This was before she met and married your father, Hans the Tinker, and got for her troubles the whole of Europe, and sore feet and hands. Make yourself comfortable.

She was beautiful, as I said, the one faithful morsel whom all in the village agreed upon. Her hair was the colour of corn-silk and easily as soft; her skin was unmarked, evenly graced by the sunformed adorable freckles at the bridge of her nose, the vase of her throat, and so on. Her hands were of the nimblest and most elegant trim and her lips as red as the flash of a blackbird's wing. She got under everyone's heart when she moved, the last curve of the road before home, and one summer she ripened. I do not know how to describe it, except to suggest that she *opened* in a grave and musical way——the way a pea-pod will split when it attains its sweetness in truth, a pea so sweet...

But this is a subject best left to your mother. On with the tale, before I lose it.

At the end of that summer, after a literal barrage of suitors, who pretended to be liberal too—indeed, there was a scraped-together look about some of the getups, as if they were leftover loot from a war unheard of in these parts—some with passion and wit, some with money, young men with muscles and utter bewildered confusion at your mother's beauty, your mother, overwhelmed, most heartsick took a walk out of the village along the crest of the three-treed hills and thence to the white and winding path that led into the large and dark forest——a path with caves, that flirted with following the tricky river. It had been late afternoon when she set out; a chill was on her bare legs as she walked briskly along the plush last heat of the earth. She knelt and covering her eyes, made a wish. She wished she would find her own true love and set out, again, of a firmer, lighter heart, despite the presence of old, lost locusts in the forest and the possibility to consider of snakes. Oh and she was young and fearless, with the cold dark leaves around her and the sturdy trunks, she would walk all evening through the forest to the meadow where the dusty bees bounced, from clover to clover.

She'd think about the bees later.

In a little while, however, she was tired of the white path and its meanderings and sat by its side on a rock, not far from the invisible river. As one does when tired, she tried to remember the purpose of her journey. It was hard. She could not. She could picture the spot, purple-and-patched in the hills where they said Kepler had pitched his tent to be near the stars. She remembered the cloven entrance to the woods, and the first pleasures of the path—the mushroom ruffles and lifted trills of the eyes, birds—but she was tired and alone and when she lifted her head from her knees, she gasped, he was so near her.

But it was not Kepler. Instead there stood in fine leather boots a handsome young man and his black cloak, an old metal-braced book in his arm, which he shifted, so as to take or shake her hand. She looked a long time and stared at his face, not insensitive, not unfeminine, before he spoke and she spoke and they both blinked.

"I am Hilda, from the village."

"Johann." His eyes were blue. "From far away." Too blue. "I am a genius."

It went on. It transpired. She was increasingly suspicious of him as he talked. He explained that he was travelling because his soul was young though the world was old and there was much he had not seen yet and little time to see it. When she asked him, quite politely I should say, what he would like to see, he laughed, and took her arm, and led her back along the white path and out of the forest, and there, on the slope of the hill, they watched a small band of villagers threshing by torchlight; beating the very red sparks out of the earth. From a distance they beheld it, holding their breaths. He said he liked to watch the people work, and wished indeed that he could lead such a simple life, but alas, he had much to do, to see, to think about, many things to set down in his book, which he tapped on lightly through his cloth hat.

"Well, you can't watch me," she said.

She crossed her arms and pouted.

They said goodbyes, and parted, she down the hill to home, to turn and lose his shape in the starry inclinations of the sky—but she thought he bowed, once. Then there was only the sound of the wind and clip-clop of a rider off, somewhere, beyond the village.

That was the first time your mother met him, Goethe, when he said he was a genius. Do not think by the way I am very impressed by his admission, or definition. It is ludicrously easy to think these things sometimes, especially if you are a young man in the company of such a lovely girl as your mother was. And she was always very difficult about this part of the story. Once she claimed that Goethe had only said he was *generous*——and she had cut him off. But in general she stuck to the genius version. As I have tried to make plain, it was a summer of some swelling, my dumpling.

For Hilda's father, your grandfather, was not amused at supper. "Thinks he's smart," he snapped.

I will not bother to report the ensuing argument, rife as it was with anger, tears, judgements and commandments, references to good clerks and tax collectors, credits and debits, and the primacy of the Bible as reading matter; suffice it to say it broke up at last with a furious and fevered Hilda slamming her door and flinging herself on her bed, where she cried herself to sleep. The next morning a swallow's importunity awoke her, and she was deeply tired, a disastrous fatigue that would culminate in her betrothal to Hans, who, we know now, was no happy remedy for downtroddenness!

Three days later she returned to the large dark forest. She left at night. She stayed far too late. Her parents grew anxious, then alarmed. I am afraid this part exceeds my skill——I perforce must merely sketch the cries and threats of Hilda's father, the urgent beckoning of friends, the torches and horses and the speed with which the searchers galloped into the woods and, calling separated, fanning out in the leafy shadowlanded gloom, smaller and smaller, until their voices and their flickering fires were thin, like insects ticking along the surface of snowy rock and rivulet.

However, for Hilda the evening passed pleasantly enough. She found herself unafraid in the wood and walked with a sure step to the heart of the dark, and softly called to him.

"Come on up."

Goethe was reading in the fork of an oak tree. He offered her his hand as her pretty face poked up near his knee. His cloak, smelling strangely of planets and vapours, draped over a stumpy knob. He read to her for a while from his book. Then there was quiet. They heard the trampings and stampings, saw the torches and horses, but so far below them they couldn't be bothered. When the leaves above them grew silvery green, very delicately down they jumped and he led her back to the village. He had to hoist her through her bedroom window, a feat for which neither was prepared and were both too silly and delirious to resist, so he heaved, and she plopped over the sill, her skirt hooked on her ears. By the time she got back to the window, he was gone, and again she heard a hoof thunder, fainter and fainter, through the excellent fabric of her skirt and her hair.

And this, my sweet, is where your mother's story grows formless and takes on a sort of sorrow. Her father found her; enraged and rash, he had her marry the next man who asked; twenty minutes later, I don't care, he's not here, Hans the Glans was at their door, selling scissors. She married, had children, forgot about many things, but not about the young man in his cloak who said he was a genius.

Many years passed.

Then, one autumn, your mother was hunting for mushrooms on the fringe of the forest, when she heard sleek hounds baying a ways off. These were the King's own hounds, they were fierce and courageous and when she heard them a measureless panic took hold of her, she fled, she ran faster and faster into the woods. She stopped, panting, panting. A golden deer stepped from behind a tree, gently regarded her, and spoke. It was lovely and truly a golden deer, and very frightened. "Soon it will be dark," it said to her, "and I will not be able to see. Take this hat——" and it flipped a black battered hat at her——"and get me some matches, please." Which she did. Avoiding the King's hounds she made it back to the village, to the candlemaker's shack and showed him the hat. He was a fat man, and when he saw the hat and heard her request, he shook with anger, spilled a handful of matches on the counter, took great care to break each match, snap, so there was only a jagged sliver of wood, a spike, below each round, blue tip. And he dropped them one by one into the hat she held. "I think these should do," he said, "for little fires."

She reached the tricky river by twilight. She could not, exhausted, worried, find the deer. The hounds yelped still, in a line to the east. There was a splash, to end her prayers. Three swans glided out of the weeds, said *Come* to her. And come she did, she waded in and swam, kicking hard to keep the hat up, the matches dry. The three swans spread their wings and linking rings in the dark, dispersed.

She saw the cloak twirl above the bank, dark, folding as it slowed to trap his form. With whitened hair, and a face of bones, he helped her out of the water, and whispered to her shivering, and sat beside her, fingering his book.

52

It was a long time before he spoke.

"I'm inventing a machine, a wonderful machine," he said.

She shivered.

Swallows flew out of his cloak.

And very slowly she made out around them, on the dark bank his visions, a vesper-orchestra of ghosts, a mechanical plethora of earthly and unearthly shapes needing an inner life, like the forms of the stillborn, knights with their shoulders roped open bleeding sinew and dim banners, maidens at prayer on lighting-lit parquet, with their wimples rotted into veils for them, a baby crawling through far hills made of dragonfly parts, gaining on a horse whose flesh was ungaining, vanished, sudden faces of Charlemagne and Arthur and the melody of a million seasons compressed into variously successful mists.

Night. The river flows. A man and your mother sit by the river. Stars come out. She can see it is hard for him to concentrate on her; when he succeeds, it dims, the shapes dim; they brighten at each of his failures. Finally he smiles. He lets his cloak fall over her because she shivers. She watches him. His fingers lift and touch, again and again, the page he is staring at. There is a slight motion of his temples.

"Can I see your machine yet?" she asks.

"Ah," he says, "It is a very slow machine."

Today is the thousandth birthday of our village.

Kildonan Park

When people ask me—and it isn't often

that they do——where did you grow up? *learn* something? the question floors me. Always will. The years back there, for me, they compare themselves in memory so mildly. They are rarefied zones, of education, of budgeted journeys, of meaningless loves and needs, which there is a need for, granted.

But in Kildonan Park I learned something more.

It was in the very north part of Winnipeg, before the quaint wreckage of Old Kildonan and the lovely candle-factory near Selkirk. Before the graveyard and the schoolboys of Saint John's in their brick school, who lived there, snowbound, and in the autumns were rosy-cheeked hawking apples and honey from their rusty Flyer wagons. I suppose that yearly trip to the city must have been no less than epic for them; that was how their characters were being built, according to the school's literature. They fanned out and pleaded at doors all over North Winnipeg, which was known to be hostile to the door-to-door. The bus to Templeton (the sewer loop; sanitation works were nearby) was $.15 and that's what I got a week for allowance. I never took the bus because I lived next door to the Park. I became a hunter and gatherer there. Six and a half acres for $.15. And the real money was in the Park. I held onto the coins and spent a lot of time there.

It seemed safer.

At the time.

Other places were, in fact, more dangerous. We damn near exploded a truck once with a shoddy campfire at the Sanitation Works. That was prime. A kid's body had been found, water-logged and shy of green in the bulrushes past Salter, so very few of us ventured there. Even in Margaret Park in the mud-mountain construction sights there were bands of mean boys (Indian, Ukrainian, Anglo-something) on wheelie bikes with cobra bars; they would line a hill of sand in the evening so their fenders and chains glinted, their frames and manes. If you looked at them they threw stones at you.

No, I played in the Park.

Sometimes I spent the $.15 at Slivovitz's —he was a bald Jew whose apron-string was too high-in-the-back-of-his-neck, and among shelves of dusty tomato soup he handed me a bag of junk and I went outside and behind the billboard started eating from it. I was happy. I suddenly felt very fond of baseball and wanted to play; with a stick and a few rocks I batted a few over the billboards onto Main Street. It didn't take long for a friendly cop to show up.

"Kid," he said. "Kid... do me a favour. Play in the Park."

I began by hunting golf balls on the fence-trails near the back nine. The bushes blotted out the sun, I'd scuttle and run to pounce on them, The Slazengers and Nicklauses and Top-Flites, white or virulent yellow eggs in the dirt. Then it got harder; the game was to sell them back to the golfers. When you hoarded, you gained leverage.

"That ain't my ball."

"So play another."

"Okay."

"Two dollars."

I poked the balls through the fence. The player would swear violently——no small thrill——and poke bills through, or bill. Twos were a prize.

But there is no use explaining some things: there was a house in the middle of the nine surrounded by trees and by baseball backstops, utterly sealed off from golf balls——yet the windows were often smashed.

How hard those golfers must have tried to smash them, to hit that hard ball harder and reach the house.

It also had a picket fence, and had been the old cottage of the first gameskeeper, the employee of a Lord, who had pot-shotted at poachers before, after and, likely, during the first world war. I didn't know that then. And it would have helped to explain why the Harpers——we think it was them, then again, we will never know——why they put a rope smeared with shit across our porch after my Dad told them never to cross our yard. I heard him chew them out why I was mixing mud around in the birdbath. He had it wrong. The Harpers never cut across yards. They played in their own yard, which was full of shopping carts and vagrant newspapers. The rope stayed in my Dad's head for a a long time.

A tiny shock: these kids, the Harpers, are crossing the verge of the creekgrass and it's morning towards the Armstrong Street Gate, and they break down the lip of the creek and stonestep it and work hard up the third bank, practically on their hands and knees.

Glen Bell and I are hidden in bushes. Glen can no longer restrain himself; he leaps up, shouting, "You goddamned Indians. This was land that was good!"

Duane the eldest looked back, but didn't challenge us. We saw their backs. We stayed hidden. Glen got a book out of the Woolco bookmobile which was an *Illustrated Children's History of*

Scotland. The Bells were Irish, and Glen thought this Scottish stuff a great improvement, and became zealous. Heads together, we chanted all the italic verses in the history.

> *Scots wa hie wi Wallace bled*
> *Scots wa hie wi Wallace dead*
> *Lead us to your gory bed*
> *Or to victory!*

It was our infatuation, and you may infer ours was a racist neighborhood. As Scots we had plenty of enemies, the Balutas, the Kowbells——"That's a change in that name," Glen said, his mouth clamped on a sharp stick, "they used to be Kowbelskis. They are the worst liars."

Glen was brash but when I think of his playground feats (his *modus*, sneakily deployed, was to jump a smaller kid from behind and stuff snow in his face) Burns, not Wallace, comes to mind: Glen Bell was a "Wee, timorous, cowering beastie."

One Saturday my Dad called me into his study. I would soon refer to him as Father, but, for the moment, he sat there with a brown and flashbulb-yellow portrait of Jesus and a wall-ankh panelling him.

"What is this?" he said, and placed a letter I had written, and mailed, to Glen on the coffee table.

"A letter."

He began to read from it. "Our fort on that day will be by Swimming-Pool and we will stay their fire by our engines and rifles. Many shall we slay, and many shall go down to doom wi' it."

A terrible smile had started to creep up in me, and I opened my mouth and said, "I'll never do it again," and went outside to have a visit with my scooter.

Well I whizzed up and down the backlane hill a couple of times, and came to the conclusion he was mad at me, but it was still about the binoculars. There were a couple of older kids smoking a cigarette against a garage door. Another friend of mine named Sebastian had them; he lived by the Red River, next to the flood pump station, and he wasn't going to give them back. I was afraid of him. He was bigger and more insulting than I would ever be. Already with Father I had begun making excuses: "Sebastian wants more time with them." I knew they were expensive. Golf would end soon too. I knew I'd have to jack my gold ball prices through the roof to pay for the binocs; but, as it turned out, they were unreachable at any price.

It was a great surprise when I received an air-rifle for Christmas. I spread back the wrapping and just looked at it for five minutes, then lifted and cradled it, tracing the dark metal and wood with my fingertips and gave my Father a long and questioning look——forgiveness? But he seemed, or it seemed, rather, that those embarrassments and criminal negligences were all behind him, though I did not entirely rule out amnesia.

I took a mock shot at him.

He smiled, laughed, *feebly*, put his hand up, and ducked. Slow. He was dead a minute ago. I dressed like a little robot in parka and earmuffs and pretended, rather sillily, for my mother, to load the gun at the back door, chewing off a plug of some antique explosive powder while she adjusted my scarf, and held the door open for me, I was in winter the wonderland of my gun and well bundled up as I walked down Ord toward the Armstrong Gates and the dark green log cabin beyond, the roof lolloped white, the pines, too, dressed. A sandspreader all invincible slow metal passed on Armstrong. I sighted it, and silently fired. Then I planted the shaft of my rifle in the snow crust and arm-vaulted the gate, my scarf falling off. I drew the gun under the gate into my wet mitts.

I walked to the mouth of the creek-culvert. I would shoot a rat, I was certain. Rats lived in the miles and miles of culvert that led to the Main Street sewer. Main Street was visible from the creek, but it was a lot of snow, six football fields, I would have bet, to crawl under.

The grey and icespiked hole I broke the frazel of its lip-pond and stirred the water with the tip of the rifle. A rat!

Or a rabbit. Paradisiacal.

At the skating-pavilion I gave my gun to the waitress, because she sounded reassuring when she told me I'd get it back. Hot chocolate by the fire. The skaters and their scarves glided round and round the stone-lined pool.

And it wasn't half bad.

But it got worse.

The gun busted.

Even though it was an accident, Father refused to get it fixed.

The gameskeeper's place was sitting in the middle of the golf course, snow on the roof, its windows broken. A long time until the golf balls flew again.

One Sunday dinner Father brought up the binocular subject.

"Sebastian isn't finished with them," I lied. I hadn't seen him. He was using the glasses as he sat at the grand piano I knew to be in his house at a bay window with someone old and doughy in bonnet and lace in attendance, bearing him tea.

"This Sebastian, then, does he like birds?"

"Loves them. Adores them. Seb and the birds."

"Don't talk like that with your mouth full."

I finished my rice pudding feeling improved by it and retired to my room and began thinking. On my knees I looked deep into the pocket of my baseball glove.

Next day I was at school early and whistling for Billy Homenick over the schoolyard asphalt. The whistle barely reached him, for he was on the girls' side watching the girls' play. He walked all the way around the fence to meet me. We stood with our hands in our pockets and I talked. Very intentional soccer balls whizzed past our toques.

"Billy, man, you've got to see my raft," I said.

"You have a raft?" He spit out a ju-jube and mopped a thin hair back.

"Yeah, me and the old man used to go all over Scotland with it. And then on it we assailed the Atlantic, we came over."

"Get out."

"Listen, Billy, honest to God I did. He's my real father."

"Is he here?"

Billy was bleating. He banged his mitts. Fat kids are usually very cold and they blubber; they become goggle-eyed at new beliefs. They share their ju-jubes. "Wow," he said.

"I need money to lay in provisions," I found myself saying to a kid unaware that, had I binoculars, I would have occasionally espied him with them but never have gone near him. "We're going. Down the Red. I know where the raft is parked, and he's waiting for me, but he doesn't want my parents to find out about us, and I sure don't and I can't have him go get the flour and the coffee—"

"You drink coffee? Wow," Billy said.

"All the time, black, but you see he can't do it; he'd say 'Have the coffee gotten up in the wee tins, laddie,' and that'd wreck it, they'd be suspicious. If you give me some money I'll show you the raft."

"How much?"

"Ten dollars." It was a start. Later I could ask him to get

59

more provisions, Lucky Charms or Honeycomb or Pop-Tarts—this was great.

"Ken Dryden is a fag," a kid in a big, big Hudson's Bay coat said to me. He had evidently come all the way across the playground alone to let us know that.

"Bugger off," I said.

"I can get you ten from my job, a week, my papers," Billy thought out loud. He also slobbered. "But I want to see the boat first."

"Oh, I don't know."

The playground teacher had hold of the flag lines, raising the Maple for the morning bell, which was in her mitten and ringing gently as she tugged and tugged. She was married to a fireman. Think, I thought, think.

"Okay," I said.

For no idea had come.

I suffered immensely for two days with my spelling primer. I was learning how to spell *ould* and *ght*, but I couldn't have been further from being caught up with *ought* and *could*; they could wait. On Friday after school we set out under auspicious winter-evening clouds. I told my parents we were at a movie; that was Billy's idea; most, if not all, of his ideas came from movies; I'd seen him work Godzilla into the most unlikely conversations.

I couldn't get out of it, everything I did from now on would only dig me deeper into it. We trudged across the field of wet, shining snow near the River Gate, *right in front of Sebastian's bay window*: how powerfully I wanted to stop! We did stop, briefly, near the empty swimming pool and I thought of how many and what green kind of diseases I could get, quicklike. It was far too warm for hypothermia.

Down the monkey trails we went, under the rope bridge and the toboggan slide's log palisades and past the kitschy witch's cottage.

"I, don't, believe, in witches," Billy said, ahead of me, huffed out.

A minute later I shouted, "Boo!" and Billy shot porpoise-like into a fall of willow branches, smashing them flat; he thrashed on his back. They tinkled and shook as I freed him.

The track veered north along the river.

Billy pulled up his pants.

How cruel I was, and incapable!

Billy tried to tie his boots and had trouble, had to plonk on his backside to get them done.

Lose him, get him lost, pretend to be lost myself, lead him, nevertheless, back to safety, save him, collect the ten dollar reward that would surely be offered.

Mastermind! You have brilliantly set the spot on the bank's location in doubt and led this fat boy to a mythical raft, perhaps his death, and it's twilight. You had a problem? No problem. I mean, Show me the problem! I laughed out loud when Billy leapt into the air, scared of a squirrel. Better. River getting very dark, things against the snow stood out, shadows flickered. The golf course fence ended at our root-toeing, boot-filled steps and we looked over the still water of a low area, a winter swamp. A single bird hopped from stone to stone with a mechanical eye on us. Things were essentially terrifying, or getting that way: we heard noises, faint barks, ice cracked, a moaning wind I could not have imagined better came up behind us. Billy was clearly influenced; he stopped, his hand on a crack in the neck, and looking way up, one-chinned, through the trees. A simple wisdom came upon him:

"It's getting dark."

"It's just a little farther. Go on, lead."

The growth and whip-stings against our cheeks were thicker here, to be pulled back and let go, smarted and tasted, and because I was behind I bore the brunt of this. Injustice. Up a rise, down a dip we worked in shadow and crossed the spur-tracks and looked together across the Bridge of Old Kildonan. The eastern shore was lit in small patches a hundred yards above the bank—the first apartment lights of the evening. Our shadows must have streaked across the river at that moment, lost, not wanting to let on. We spoke a few words to each other. I kept it crisp. This was no time for some clumsy oath of friendship.

"How much farther is it?"

"Not much."

"How far is it?"

"You want to see the raft, don't you? Don't turn back. I'm sure it's up ahead."

"I don't know," he said.

"Are you scared like a little baby?"

"You bet I'm scared."

To my surprise he set out again in a rugged, wobbling fashion. I did not particularly want to bring violets to Billy in Miseracordia, and that's what I concentrated on principally while I caught up with him. He crushed through a dam which I vaulted

61

—beavers here?—and pitched towards the river.

We came out together on the bank.

Inspiration.

I must have seemed insane. I babbled. I grabbed him. I pointed, pointed. "They took it! They took it!"

"Who? Who?"

"The robbers, it must be the robbers."

"Robbers?"

Billy was helpless.

I stopped thinking. I swept my arm north and said, "Oh, the robbers who live over there. Billy Billy Billy, the old man was afraid of this!"

Billy looked where my hand went and turned white.

Can't blame him.

The tombstones of the Old Kildonan Jewish Cemetery and its ancient mausoleum came down to the river, to people the few black treetrunks and crepuscular stumps, as if they had strolled down, stones, or drifted. They had walked out of these last trees on purpose, off-white, carved in Hebrew characters, too numerous, too forlorn for the mausoleum. The characters were names and what is it about Hebrew writing? The stone's word had been left by a highly trained flame. And Billy and I, remembering our yell and a piece of the sky, ran home.

I knew I'd never see the binoculars or Billy again.

But it didn't matter. There were years left, plenty of them, summers to be in the monkey tree and dreamily watch the teenagers kick field goals. My allowance went up and there were long bus rides to the Stadium, where I sat in the Salisbury End Zone with soggy hotdogs and watched the Bombers vying in the ties of autumn, footballs spinning on the muddy grass. When I was babysat, be still my heart, by babysitters in jeans and beads, the whole thing was over, the kids in the stone-throwing gangs were placing Led Zeppelin forty-fives on tiny stereophones in Community Club Basements and a few of the girls on Newton Street were confirmed at last, as girls as well as Catholics. Boys started seeing them. The Bell house had a light on many nights, late, and once, when the girl in tears returned, Mrs. Bell stood out on the sidewalk and swiped at her daughter with a broom, in front of the whole neighborhood, and called her a whore. I have since heard the Irish intonation described as musical; it has made me feel sorry for that very broom.

I met up with Billy again when he started ushering at the

Odeon, still fat in a popping uniform.

"Hi, Billy."

He tore my ticket. "Hi. Let me know if the flick's good."

"I went to see the Guess Who in Kildonan Park last weekend."

"Cool. Good?"

But then he had to lead a couple to their seats and he plodded in front of them in the red cone of his little flashbeam. Right handed, I saw.

I am left handed myself, still a liar. I live in a kingdom to the west now, where around industrial parks there are moats, and clock towers in the centre. And last week, what do you know? I heard on the radio there were a couple of cases of the bubonic plague reported in the Fraser Valley, near Mission. I presume they were treated. If not, they're dead, and they will never betray me.

Pictures of Istanbul

The city's name, perhaps, is heard with

fresh force far to the north-west, in a region where the fields are stony and the land in general a cold, hard blue. It is what a man who stands beside a bus shouts, Is*tan*bul, and it sounds marvellous, all hoarse stress; activity (bags shoved under, steps mounted, shoes, boots, shoes, tickets clutched) surges about the bus at its repetition, IsTANbul, a rise to a shout on that syllable generic and directional.

Gravel is steadily crunching, the bus fills and its windows fog; to and fro in the windows of the lighted ticket shops faces come and go. The name is shouted a last time, the man swings himself up at the rear doors as the bus roars and wheels out of the circular cement moonlight to rock down a rutted drive and hunch up on the highway's smoother pavement, where it starts to pick up speed "to the city".

This is not far from the border of Greece, a neighbor, where the city is known by another name. It has had several: conveying, variously, magnificence, centrality, the imperial, the transcendent, emnity, unity, the decadent, the holy. And indeed it is tawdry and eternal, just as, in different times and in different ways, it has stood as door between West and Europe and East and Asia and then and now. To say I am going there and mean I am going there is quite impossible. Complicated explanations are required; bridges and vantages important.

An inhabitant posing the most simple of all ideas, that of living in a modern country, if speaking to a foreigner, soon discovers that no foreigner considers the city or country modern absurd!—and will persist in this prejudice no matter how many perfectly reasonable measures are proposed. So the inhabitant keeps his idea of modernity to himself, a frustration.

The visitor, pressing the most vivid of all wishes, that of living in an ancient city in an ancient land, finds not only that people live in the present but also that, considered abstractly, the city 's antique charm can only persist in monuments, the sculpted contagions of ideas no longer really living: their time has died around them and they are too easily contradicted. So the visitor keeps his ideas to himself, as photographs.

The city is wilful, of surfaces weaving and ending, alembic, living and bending. There are any number of perspectives, the hungry poor supported by their bones in frozen swamps, in airplane interiors tailored sophisticates, from which to anticipate the city.

The people on the bus, enjoying the smoke, the cologne on thin faces, and the crowded heat, experience it first as a widening of the highway, an evident series of flashes, lights on faster cars passing. And gradually the highway is more strongly lighted and there are more and more slow, swinging stops on the shoulder, passengers who step off. The buildings here are rude concrete shells. Some of their windows are broken. Loops of live wire are hung from spikes on the telephone poles. There are no crowds at these first stops, only, when the windows are wiped clear, a few poorly dressed men, some hefting barrows and wheeling these by long handles, and the departed passengers striding briskly away, bag held, other hand in pocket, for the night is cold. Through the mix of moistures against glass when they press their faces to it, there comes on them a depth of prospect, as of neighborhoods never-been-before in: the buildings, cheap, looking molded rather than built, the chipped, the stained, the painted-on and sometimes crumbling or smashed-in concrete, plaster and a vaporous mixture of these, the dark, small cluttered windows and the flat rooves, many-aerialed, littered with trash, discarded furniture, shapes, and the steps fronting offices, and boys or young men dallying, knees drawn up, who watch with interest too, back at the passengers, little, but some interest, but not as in some other place (like where they are heading), immediately leaping to offer service; the buildings continue, proliferate, their slow trickle of signs, and the signs themselves, printed signs, trades and goods and ownership, misspelled or else stolen from the hand, the sporadic and sporelike, unyielding light attached to (admittedly) poorly lit tiles —this depth of prospect is more than the bleak, the homogenous, the mist-in-mid-air apparition of simple streets and shreds of laundry, more than the isolated pockets of all downtrodden towns but is instead the face of something larger that makes the bus a tunnel running through an outside rumble, the stutter of sensed but unknown lives. There is a general excitement. The passengers are in the city now and it will go on for at least another half an hour. Some wipe harder at their windows; they try to see more. At another stop there is a large lokanta and the smell of cooking food slowly penetrates the bus. And then they sweep upward; the neighborhoods curtainpeaked displays of light and darkness from which green and brilliant soccer fields leap square and expansive from behind chimneys; a lone minaret crosses the window. The highway is four or five lanes now, streams out ahead, dives and keeps downward. There are so many car lights, so many car sounds, tires, horns, motors. Billboards, factories, traverse avenues. It is necessary now for the driver to shout out neighborhoods, the usual stops. Far ahead, ranging, hilly at the end of the electric crawl of traffic is the familiar outline of the city proper, which at least takes its shape from the slowly inching lights at its edge, cars moving completely around its form like a paper tissue's slow patrol of non-entity as it burns to crisp whisps, nothing in a clear bowl, and the city slopes to shape the black water, which glints, the towers are sunken loose cones of gold flake. On the bus, completely involuntary gasps, people up merely to push their baggage around on the overhead racks, reassure themselves it is still there. The highway dips again, the bus races past sheds, fences, areas, stacks, pyramids towards a dark horizontal apparently separating a lower from a higher field of windows, a wall. Then vision is blocked: virtually all stand and pull down bags, jackets, boxes with rope handles, and the bus slows, and it turns, and it stops. Many light new cigarettes and one by one step down on gravel again.

It is but a short walk, dodging and hustling to the gates in the wall, an old fortification. The light through the gates plays, dances; once through, it is seen to be the limber effect of fires in oil drums. A violent, punching release of smell, and a noise writhing, glisting in the air against stone. Though there was radio music on continually in the bus, this compels, these are irresponsible gusts, they swirl, they are emotional, Arab, the singer's voices ululate an infinite variation, curled and intricate, on an arid interval. Near the fires the cassette decks blare, set on hoods above grilling meat, roasting nuts; and the vendors' faces are set to receive, they are dark and old. The crowd begins to branch and veer, many stops and starts are necessary, the voices of the vendorwomen in enveloping robes are at once needy and remote. It is very easy to trod unwittingly on someone's blanket strewn with watches, pens, amulets, combs or on someone else's leg, who is begging, not selling. The fires torque. The drivers of the cars for hire push off their fenders and walk around their vehicles, get in, wait. Overhead, distant, rising and climbing, the call to prayer winds, cries and twines, again rising, hiking higher as each other high-pitched, over-lapping shriek joins in, from farther and farther away, held, and hurled, highwiring, a trapeze of desire above the crowd, the lights and each individual filament of that net, very thin in its pride of altitude, each one by one lessening and are quieter, less planetary as the one last voice ends and lands in traffic

patterns, the pattering rain on the Millet Caddesi.
This but an arrival at night.

In the city there are nearly as many statues of a former leader, a modern leader, as there are mosques. Though the statues (equestrian, lawgiver) are cheaper, the mosques take up more space, thus limiting the available space for further statue-venues, an enthusiasm check. Given the avowedly secular nature of the government, it is not clear what the meaning of this supercessional race is, or might be, or result may be, other than the steady blurring of the words "tradition"——*gelishme*——and "progress" ——*gelenek*——which have as their common root the particle "to come". Nuance is again directional, item altering the flow.

Morning, from a hillside overlooking the waters and the city, from an outwardly temporary but quite permanent and poor part of "the Asian side". Woodsmoke and creosote: the wood has been gathered from demolition sites in the surrounding, steep streets. The sun is behind the child; he sits outside the family shack on the gentle, green hillside. He looks down over poplars across the waters, straight between the opposable bones of banked earth the city is constructed on, seeing first the shape of the first bridge, and the old walls to the south which surround the extensive palace, the many domes and minarets which rise out of the southern slope, seeming to crown out of leaves. Already with fresh white washes the ferries ply the passage. To the north he takes in the rectangular tops of office buildings, apartments. Behind all of this there are blurrier edges, the great smoke and the solid noise, as of a worrying shunt, always. Clouds are massing to cover and fix what he sees: and then, behind him, staggered, God's words in that other language begin to repeat: distant, they begin as well over the swells in the water, coming from every point he can survey (he tosses a stick at a chicken and he laughs, delighted, the chicken blasts up, ruffles, hops, walks jerky walk) far back, forever back, vast as the haze that yellows from the city and touches and darkens the full grey ceiling. He paddles his fingers in the cooling mush of his dish of oats. His mother yells, *Put on your coat*; he ignores her. There is always another voice to make out, if he strains, and he is not very cold. A film of light lights, skips on the waters; he sees dots move on the first bridge, larger dots, then smaller, crossing, continuing. He knows he is looking from "sea" to "sea", one visible and the other not, but easily confirmed by the large ships set here

68

and there in the water, like buildings themselves. God's words have altogether ceased and again he can hear the city, grey and knocking and green and drilling and gold and hammered and black, "a speaking cloud."

With a flushing wash and a juddering shriek of engines pulling backwards, the stern of the ferry swings in and hits, lowering and righting, and the commuters, too hurried to wait, vault the tow ropes and step quickly over the Eminönü docks. They ignore the man who is trying to fasten the tow-rope—he drops it and curses them with his hands. They plow purposefully across the asphalt space, crumpling and dashing their spent tickets down. A lottery-seller turns and turns on his yell, as they split and divigate around him, *Ön milyön, ön milyön*. The crowd veers, packed in hornless panic as they do so, now trying to avoid the simit sellers madly steering their carts in their direction. A few sacrifice the minute and fish in their large pockets for change. There are a few drops of rain and a few look anxiously at the sky. Then they are all lined up on the curb of a broad avenue where traffic sweeps; one, and two, they plunge off, a gaggle, a lone athlete twists out, slowing, then sprints across. Horns blow. The people break through the traffic that breaks through the people and they are in the city.

West, the great face of a mosque and its blocklong staircase is the gathering place; at the doors men nudge off their shoes to begin their ablutions in chatting groups while all along, up and down the steps, others read the morning papers, smoking, until the papers are folded ruefully, too soon, and they begin to walk in the morning crowds. They turn south, uphill.

The sidewalks are narrow and uneven; there are sudden concealed drops down a few steps into basement stores. The men wear either short, leather jackets or heavy kneelength overcoats with the additional adornment of a nearly brimless cap. The women favor raincoats, small groups of them wear headscarves. Everyone hurries. They take an overhead walkway and skip steps on the way down, hug a corner, and break across another street with their heads forelowered and their hands invariably in their pockets. The women (to generalize) go straight to work; the men crowd into the çay shops to stare at the popular TV programs which feature beautiful women who greet them with the customary *İyigünler* and then host mini-documentaries on this or that commendable enterprise. The men absently clink their spoons in the little tulip-shaped glasses they then drain down and, with a glance at the screen, hunch into their coats and out onto the street again.

Near the water the shopwindows burgeon with cheap imported goods: radios, pens, watches, ledger-books, cameras, umbrellas, makeup; near the defunct train station the windows darken with grime and the doorways are grilled and barred. The goods here are a tumble of bulk: engine parts flung with greasy cloth, bolts of cheap material, dusty sacks of staples.

The streets sweep upward, cobbled and potholed, towards the palace and its grounds. It is a museum, a display of wealth, of gardens and pavilions and great halls, a wall above which the tops of the trees are still, for there is no wind, only the pressing threat of the rain and the mist and fog off the Sea of Marmara. The streets level out past the palace's front gates. Groups of young men jostle one another outside shops that sell wholesale leather goods, jackets, which they all wear. They don't wear caps, or any headgear, but they will, by and by. About a block from here are military guards around a police complex armed with semi-automatic weapons.

The profusion of different streets in this area, still north of Divan Yolu—the Way of the Chancellory, as it is quaintly called, and might more aptly be called Where the Tourists End Up—reflect their international clientele with conspicuous English signs advertising Chips, Burgers, Turkish Food Here, but some do not. Some are dingy and canyonsided with lightless facades and whatever activity there is at street level does not allure, consisting of racks of clothes hauled out and leaned against windows no matter what the season, persisting in the vigilant white-jacketed smoke breaks of kitchen help who crouch on the sidewalks, in the armwaving conversation of bearded older men in hole-bellied sweaters, and of tea boys desultorily returning from their rounds, dandling their pendant trays of stained glasses, their nests of spoons. The human traffic here has slowed, and when people pass one another, there is now time (it is about nine o'clock), both walking backwards for one, two steps, for an exchange: *Gunaydin, ya Mustafa, nasilsiniz?*

Cok iyim, tessekürler, ya siz?

Ben d'yim.

And one has to sidestep, *affedersiniz,* a man who is walking slowly and close to the walls, looking at nothing in particular. He does not reply to the apology. He talks no more than is strictly necessary in the mornings. He roams offhandedly, fingering, then

70

buying a paper——usually one with either soccer player's gesticulation or a singer with a hard-to-fasten kimono as its feature photo—but sometimes the closely printed, more serious political paper. His manner is cool, his eyes morose. His beard has grown dark through the swath of his razor; his face is severe, not dashing, not romantic, just angular, the face of a man who washes daily in freezing rapids. But this man has never left Istanbul.

He stands on a corner, head bent in his cupped hands, lighting a smoke.

He will walk up one flight into one of the darker, grubbier çay shops where the windows are yellow with nicotine and he will insult the boy who is washing the morning load of glasses, as a matter of course. He will be brought his tea, and the television will be turned on for him, but he pays it no attention: he drinks the tea, his head low, and watches what passes on the street. If there are merchant marines at another table he might listen to their sporadic, bragging exchanges, their hopes for upcoming, longer stints of work, Vancouver, or more routine tasks, coal, there and back, Zonguldak. He will get the boy's attention again: *Bakar misiniz?* And when the boy, angry now, but stiffly polite, comes to his table he will smile, Good boy, you're not deaf. Then this man will slowly read the paper.

At lunch he will walk on the same side of the street as the armed guards past a tall foreign couple, one probing in the other's backpack, and bump them. He fields the immediate brusque retort smarmily, then, because he sees the object they search for is a map, he will give generous and explicit directions to the foreigners, he waves, he points, he grabs a forearm, and he lets him feel his grip; he keeps smiling; they have to thank him.

Then he buys a *börek* from a street vendor and walks through the gates of the palace into Gulhane Park where there is a small, foul-smelling zoo. He chooses a bench directly across from the common sparrows and the domestic cats and chews his food, listening with pleasure to the birds' frenzied chitter and squawk.

As the cats pace and pad.

He is employed.

Sa'im had a problem with an urgent speed inside him. It often made him look, even when doing nothing, hasty or dithering. This was exagerrated by his cramped and cold office space. In windows overlooking the street he meticulously sized portrait photos. He would line it up, bring the cutting edge down, stand, take the

71

photo out, line it up again, cut halfway along this edge, then finish it quickly with the heel of his hand, chop. As the squares of faces were shook across the table into a manypointed heap, occasionally a memory-face would dislodge itself and float up at him. One such of his father angry at him in a pastry shop. He did not have much work to do: things were slow, there were not too many tourists in the winter. The greater part of his business was to sit around and wait for the next uniformed man to tromp up the stairs and sit on his stool. His term of occupation had shrunk from the inept but colourful vistas of flowerbanks (Those ravening blurs of sun-struggling colour!) and the more commonly visited monuments (minarets lopped off) to the human face's black and white fixities. Passport size. The policemen and soldiers needed their I.D. updated because they were the official recipients of promotions, transfers, the hard gruel of a provincial tour. They were curt with him, though Sa'im was careful not to ask too many questions. He knew he was in competition with the local mosque for the portrait trade; they offered the same service, but charged more and were often sloppy. It was no great feat to do better than the local imam. Perhaps the officers talked to him.

He swept the clipping-strips off his desk and dropped them in the wastepaper basket. Then he slid the pictures into their respective envelopes. He turned down their flaps when they were sorted and sat down and leaned back behind his desk. He made some meaningless eye contact with the poster of the pretty Japanese figure skater who was affixed (Fuji Colour) to his door. The electric heater made wheezy, fusty sounds at his feet, an ovaloid metaloid pet dog.

The muezzin went off, directly across the street.

The wall of windows.

And he, involuntarily, brought his hands up to the small shelf where canisters of film, flash units jiggled, nearly unhoused; they never fell, but shook. The megaphone's wail was always dire, frightening, in a direct line with his window. (They could turn it down. Could they turn it down? They could.)

Sa'im didn't mind, and likely loved, the winter because it was private time. He could sit. He could think, if he got around to it. He could take out the big Redhouse Dictionary and learn more English words. As he mouthed them (*serving-dish, forearm, bear*) the summer's babble, his beery conversations in the pubs of Sultanahmet rose towards his pursed lips from the finely printed blur of words. Someone had told him this summer, and told him

72

again, kindly, that he spoke English very well, like an American.

There was an injunction there, like an absent voice to which he kept listening: a restriction.

He drew open the drawer and felt around for the plasticized folder.

He placed it on his lap and went through his German friend's pictures, nudes on the beach at Öglü Deniz. He didn't find the women attractive; indeed, as he looked, and thumbed the photos, he was unable to resist thinking of sunburn. He liked the idea of the romp of it though—wet sand, wet women.

She'd meet him here tomorrow, Halima had said.

Did he feel like the darkroom today? It did, the day, seem to stretch ahead, rainy, not uncomfortable, but there was nothing he wanted to do. He'd taken no snaps of his own since Temmuz, when an old army koç of his had happened through Istanbul. These hardly seemed to need his developing, and there were still fifteen exposures left on the roll.

There were footsteps outside, and the Japanese girl swung goodbye to be replaced by Balid the tea-boy, in his haughty leather jacket with padded shoulders.

"*Assalaam 'alaykum*," Balid said.

"Yes, *merhaba*, Balid. One tea, *lütfen*."

Respond to this Balid wasn't about to—he stood, insolent, one hand on the doorknob, his eyes darting here and there in the small shop.

"He wants one tea," he muttered finally.

Sa'im sighed, and scrabbed up a green chit from the withheld basket. "*Hamdulillah*," Balid said. "I didn't ask you how you were," Sa'im said. "No, you never greet me as a brother should." Sa'im sighed again, and the sigh's essence of tepid release after long patience briefly misted one of the tea glasses Balid held and slowly swung over to set down on the desk.

As soon as the glass touched, Sa'im grabbed Balid's wrist. "Balid, I'm so sorry, maybe *Insha'Allah* one day I will. That day we're brothers. So today how stupid are you." "Do you have any glasses for me to take, *effendim*," Balid shook his arm free. "You took them yesterday. Remember? You went over *haram* and *halal* for me." "Yes, you make fun of *haram* and *halal*, very stupid. Bay Ozgen asked for you today." "You can tell Bay Ozgen he doesn't get another *kurush* until the toilet and the landing and the front door is fixed."

Sa'im said this very calmly.

Balid picked up and turned delicately with his tray and said over his shoulder, "The President sees what is important now, he is a wise man."

"The 'President'".

"Yes, he wants to see the headscarves on our women."

"'Headscarves.'"

"Yes, and he is a powerful man."

"The powerful man who got what a joke twenty two per cent on the referendum."

Balid blinked. Sa'im could see him formulating the appositive Arabic phrase. Not understanding "referendum" had scarcely troubled him; here it came, from the lips he carefully partitioned, "*Allahu akbar.*" And his head was between door and jamb, "Bay Ozgen has been teaching me," he said, and shut it.

Sa'im threw his hands in the air. "We recommend you to God," he said.

He drank his tea sitting on the upended and empty metal case of his portrait camera, which he used as a stool for the sessions. Then he went and stood for a moment in his darkroom, long enough to make to realize he was late and for his eyes to enable in the dim, red light and intuit shape. He stepped out, put on his coat, locked up, and began to walk to the Hürriya Pansiyon.

The square, which stretches out for long legs, broken by the two ranked replicas of obelisks, the cobbles shining, on the puddles rain flecks. Outside Aga Sophia there are only a handful of tour buses, same at Sultanahmet. The flowerbeds are bare brown going black. A man in a raincoat sits behind his crate and typewriter under an umbrella with a bent stem. The shoe shine boys walk up and taunt and down the steps behind him. They, and a few other small walking figures convey the strange improbability of the square in winter, its forgottenness.

Shoeshine boys? Incredible. But in the cafes (Pierre Loti, Pierre Loti, Pierre Loti) along Divan Yolu, fronting on the public steps and paths, there are many who will agreeably relate from shoeshine boy and on their upwards condition. Man with a vintage typewriter who taps away for pennies in a park? In a state with a public education system, surely he is no longer necessary, a deliberate antique. Do people really need someone to write letters for them, and in fastidious Ottoman phrasing? Yet he is. He needs the money.

In the sky all densities have their time above the city.

In the palace grounds the walks are slick and shiny, marble with sky wedged in it, a shadow tabula to train the eye, to sort out difference, degree, of gold a framed pavilion's filigree, of gold the winter apples of a dark-haired tree.

The Sultan's halls: male custodians in thick grey overcoats stand in front of heater. Their fingers work the worry beads behind their backs, finish, flip the beads over, begin. What few tourists there are stroll past the glass cases, booty from the past. They greet the custodians, who smile weakly back at them, with a few memorized phrases.

"*Günaydin.*"

"*Merhaba, Günaydin.*"

"*Iyigünler.*"

"*Siz günaydin.*"

"Balid, no one but God could tolerate Balid." Sa'im walked downhill as he savoured each rich sarcasm that occurred to him. "Teaching Balid." He knew what that meant. Ozgen, perhaps, no, for sure, with the help of one of those silk-suited young men was teaching Balid, patiently, to parrot what they thought. No, repeat, *tekrar, tekrariniz,* an elderly man his father had brought into their apartment in Zeyrek. Sa'im was indifferent; it mattered little to him; it mattered little whether headscarves were approved or a disgrace, in or out or on backwards. Halima often wore hers and who cared.

The newspaper cartoons had been depicting the President, who was low, abjectly so in the opinion polls, in a headscarf all week. The editors would go to jail, and be released shortly. The round of Republican publishment and punishment would begin again.

Entirely what was the point, thought Sa'im.

He backed against the wall to let an hamalca pass to stump steadily uphill under his load. Sa'im smelled coalsmoke. As if to confirm this, around the corner the familiar glistening pyramid of brown hulked coal was dumped outside the doors, halfway dug down into the underground grate. A couple of the staff were slicing at it with shovels in the rain. And the street was quiet: no children. He usually had to duck soccer balls kicked from corner to corner by kids with white-skulled, shaved heads.

In the lobby of the Hürriya the night staff were still waking up; by the sheeted windows in the bay nook they stretched, yawned.

A typewriter clicked. Hassan was holding a German grammar with one hand and pecking out the guest list for the police with the other.

Sa'im met Mehmet on the stairs up to the bar.

Mehmet rather stiffly extended his hand with a disgusted look, "Goodbye, Sa'im."

"What is this?"

Mehmet rolled his eyes, indicating upstairs. "Emin. He is drunk. And I am fired."

"You are kidding."

"No, it is better. I am going to Antalya to work for my uncle. It is a better hotel." He trailed off at "hotel" as if realizing what a perfectly absurd notion and banal comparison to make, and hefted his gymbag.

"What happened? What did you—he do?"

Mehmet smiled, and closed his eyes. Sa'im watched him down the stairs.

He caught up to him in the lobby.

Mehmet and Hassan were bent towards each other over the reception counter, whispers, tales of the inexplicable force drinking three stories over their heads.

"You need money?" Sa'im said.

"Oh, no, no, it's all right. This new hotel has four stars." He laughed. "Do not be worried."

"But your family... Hassan, what is going on?"

"Mehmet is glad to be getting away from him."

"My family will be all right, *inshallah*."

"Der hotel..." Hassan said.

"And my uncle is in Antalya, it is his hotel..."

"Maybe I will visit you."

"*Inshallah*."

The three looked at each other, wondering if there were some next step to their conversation, or at least one worth taking. Hassan bent his head and hunted to an astonishing depth for the next key to peck.

"My taxi will be here and my things I will get later," Mehmet said, sounding, in his high collared uniform, all of twelve.

Sa'im embraced him, and started up the stairs again. Not sure what to expect. He stopped and lit a cigarette on the third landing, and stood there holding his smoke. One of the cleaning-women, on her knees in one of the rooms, leaned to the door when she saw him, and closed it. Sa'im could hear the sound of an

English conversation down the hall in another room.

The bar was nearly empty, nearly freezing. Emin's pugnacious face and impressive curls were slumped over, but still well above the bar. Supported only by an elbow though. Rifat Meyvesut was speaking angrily at him from a distance of three feet, perched on a stool. The calendar poster of Ataturk was behind them, Ataturk, serene, dead, mighty, his eyebrows manicured.

Don't get involved in this, Sa'im thought.

The bar was strewn with unwashed dishes and glasses.

He saw Ali wave, and went to join him by the fogged-on windows. As Sa'im sat, Ali went from glum to grim to grin. They embraced sideways in the booth, and bussed each other.

"Good to see you, *arkadesh*," Ali said, and made it sound like a comment.

"Hello, how long has this been going on?"

"Years. Half the morning."

They sat watching TV awhile.

The Hürriya's decor had changed: instead of the black and white movieish theme Emin had gone with for a while, the entire bar was now earthbright with kilims hung on the walls, the floorspace all low tables and tiny squatting-stools and seat-pillows. Tribal weaving dominated. The marquee posters were gone. It looked uncomfortable; Sa'im was glad Ali had chosen a booth.

They heard Rifat cry out (and suppress a further shout), and then resume his tactical stridency. Emin cursed him a low doglike curse. Neither Ali nor Sa'im monitored the conversation closely; they merely reacted to its more prominent contours. Rifat Meyvesut was hammering out, it seemed, a partly etymological argument linking "brotherhood", "memory" and "the past" —which was supposed to alarm Emin about his drinking.

An antic advertisement came on the screen. Sa'im relaxed and enjoyed that his friend's arm was slung over his shoulder. They watched, with incredulous pleasure, a purposely representative Baba suffer a series of indignities: missed buses, an auto accident, his wife's latest expensive purchase: he took it all with eye-rolling resignation whereupon, safe in his washroom, Baba was seen craning and preening, just short of handsome, palms to his cheeks. "There are a lot of things I don't have to like—but I have to like my moustache," was the voiceover closure.

"That is, is so stupid," said Sa'im.

77

"The version they were working on had someone beating a simit seller to death with a donkey-leg; but what could Baba do? Just another part of life's rich texture, same as his moustache. But at least colourful. Thwack! Can't you see Baba grimace? This one's drab. A little havoc in traffic."

"Oh, go away Ali, I do not like you. I only like my moustache."

"*Effendim*, I beg you to like my moustache as much as I do."

"Ha! It is not the same. I do not have to, so I won't. What were they selling anyway."

"Skin-something clippers. Remember? The scissors."

"No."

"He missed the scissors. Effective ad."

"Yes, it is true, I missed them, but I still have my moustache."

"But do you have to have your moustache?"

"Oh, I have to, I have to! My very moustache!"

Ali laughed, lifted his coffee cup.

They listened to Rifat's voice, alone now, abstractly repeating the same injunction, "Always it must be like that, my friend, forever and ever," in a thickly rimed manner. Emin's head was definitely and heavily set on the bar, his thick eyes showing a vast, milky, reptilian indifference when he sporadically lifted his lids to comprehend Rifat.

"Everyone is leaving Istanbul, " Sa'im said.

"Everyone? Mehmet sure is... Mehmet isn't everyone, my friend."

"I will make some more coffee, if you want."

"It can wait."

Rifat edged into their vicinity, and stopped, thumbs in belt loops, his elbows pleating back his narrow lapels. He studied them, appraising their worth as audience, so it seemed that in his face there were reflected the myriad participants of a convention. Rifat scowled, deciding, after all, that they were Greek.

Ali punched Sa'im lightly on the shoulder.

"Man," Rifat managed. "I will tell you something about man, my friends."

"We want to know about Emin."

"Emin? He is not a man."

Rifat decided to ignore them; he reached for a pale, ice-melted drink on a table and swirled it. "Man is not one thing, he is many things. Sometimes it is for a man sex; he is like an animal; so he finds a woman, he has the sex. Or to drink, to eat. And sometimes he is philosophical, he wants to think, so he reads books. This is not what I am saying. I am not speaking to you of philosophy."

"Right!"

"Absolutely," Sa'im said.

Rifat snorted. "I am a realist. Emin—is he a realist? Ho!—he never remembers the past, which is like a dear brother to us. He drinks and forgets. You are intelligent men but are you realists? How realistic are you?"

"How many busboys has Emin fired this year? Seven or eight?" asked Ali.

"I do not see your point."

"Which would you say is more realistic."

Sa'im admired his friend's straight face.

Rifat sank down on a cushion, intending to say something more (or belch), but his head tilted dangerously back; he came to, placed his drink carefully on the table, and fell asleep.

"We could bundle him up," said Ali, "and take him back to his office."

"Where he will cause no disturbance."

"We should."

"I suppose you heard we didn't get it," Sa'im said.

"Our soccer, yeah. Too bad."

"I don't understand. I asked them why. They said they had given out their quota of permits."

"Yes, of course."

"If we knew someone we would have gotten it."

Erol shrugged.

"So there will be no Izmir trip."

Erol just stared at Sa'im, then said, "No."

"And we won't go to Bursa. Don't you care?"

"How can we go? We do not have a group any more."

They heard Hassan behind the bar now, placing glasses in the sink. Ali called for coffee.

"You can still play soccer. Find another team."

"Sugar?" called Hassan.

"Please, as usual," Sa'im turned, and turned back to Ali. "So, when are you leaving?"

"Tomorrow."

"You don't give me much warning. It's a good thing I stopped—no, I do not mean to be sad. But I am, a little."

79

"I am sad too."

"Where are you going?"

"I had to do something. Mersin, for a while. I'll work for my uncle."

"Who?"

"Ibrahim Misal. "

"When did you decide? What is the problem."

"There is no problem. Well there is. I can't really talk about it. If I knew myself, I would tell you. I mean if I knew what it was.

"I wasn't too surprised about our team, arkadesh. You see the way things are going. But it's not that. My family does not need me here. It's just things are ending here for me."

Hassan set the coffees down and collected the empty glasses.

"I feel I have to leave," Ali said.

Sa'im plucked at his sleeve. "You know I have that German friend. All the time he is talking about Germany. What is Germany? I do not know."

"I'm not going to Germany, just Mersin."

"I know you're not. That's not what I mean. I develop his photographs of women. And we have all those friends, Mehmet..."

"Mustafa..."

"Yes, and the whole Örtülü family, plenty of people. But what is Germany? No one can tell you what it's like."

"Sa'im, I have to go."

"No—stay."

And they did, for twenty minutes, sipping their coffees, promising to write. They got up slowly and helped each other with their coats. As Sa'im laid his money on the bar beside Emin's elbow he could visualize with stunned accuracy the rest of the evening. Hassan was nearly finished the dishes. Emin would wake up to a pristine bar, its shiny surfaces and pleasing convexities of glass and put on his tapes and dance, recklessly, passionately, tossing his curls, until Rifat woke up, woke up and said, "Many many things I have noticed about man," and watched dumbly as Emin whirled closer and closer to his safe chair, which scraped now: Rifat, in a crumpled stagger, moved towards them in the darkening bar.

"Hürriya Pansiyon. What is this word—hürriya. It means 'freedom'. What is so free about it? How can this man who cannot remember the past he is so drunk, how can he be free? Run the hotel. It is a huge joke! Huge!"

Rifat caught himself before he hit the bar. He hung by a hand from it.

"Free Emin," he said.

Then crashed, unconscious, to the floor.

Sa'im and Erol embraced outside in the fog and said good-bye.

So, thought Sa'im, there are times when it is even intolerable to be a cat.

It was drizzling out there. He returned his attention to the cat, who was taking the same two dance steps over the unmoving eyes of Özgen's body where it lay on the floor. The cat's action was obsessive, something it had decided to do and keep on doing after a brief period of panic when it had simply tried to get out of the room.

Sa'im crouched by the window, sipping grainy coffee from a styrofoam cup.

When he did decide to call Balid he got angry; as he heard Balid's petulant voice, haughty at being summoned, he blew up. Each word of Balid's met exactly his rising anger, molded to the very punchable, screw it up huck it in the corner push pin doll idea he had of Balid. Balid said he would be there directly. Good! He slammed the phone down with great relish, satisfied the same way our undertongues meet food.

He locked the door went out to eat something.

When he got back, exactly half an hour later, Balid was sitting on the stairs with his tea tray,

"Why don't you go up?" said Sa'im.

"Can't," said Balid.

Up the stairs he saw the bottom of a bathtub sized basinette working its way up into the bannisters and the set lines of risers. He called to the two men, in their suits and tarbooshes and boiled porridge beards who were doing the carrying, but they ignored him, and Sa'im tried to barge past. Balid stopped him with a hand, casually.

"These are the men who will wash him," he said.

"Just get him orada."

"They will wash him, he will go to *jenna*."

"Out, first. Then *jenna*."

And as he broke away and stumbled past them, he actually banged on the basinette, to great remonstrance from the men, and slammed into his office.

Sat there.

Listened to more bumps and bangs.

Sa'im realized that it fell to him to tell the team that tonight would be their last practise.

He was not looking forward to it.

He bought an extra pack of cigarettes on his way. He was to meet them in the kirathenese near the practise field. When he sat down with them, cleats hanging from his shoulder, Mehmed was explaining to Günesh the latest sociological-survey-cum-study he had dreamed up——he hypothesized an inversion in dwelling preference along income lines, a gradual shift towards a prestige associated with second floor living. Would people say things like,"We always felt we lorded in over those people downstairs. We had them all beat to hell. And we loved the view of the trees."

"I think you'd get a lot of people saying I've never really thought about it."

"That'd be pretty hard to dichotomize."

"It sure would. Hi Sa'im."

"*Iyiakshamlar*," he said. "What's this you're?"

"Yes, we should ask the landlords too. After all, they have some control. Were they part of a campaign to push people upstairs, or did they in fact charge more for lofty living? Don't you rent to people upstairs, hey?"

Sa'im stared at him.

Then he said, "My father rented to him. I continued to do so."

"Don't you find," said Günesh, "that your sociological studies are more and more hampered by respondents who say, 'My father did thus, and so do.' Is that a problem?"

"No, I am mostly hindered by people who do not have the slightest fucking idea of what they are doing. Which makes me uniquely qualified to engage in it. I claim special insight."

All Ayesha wanted was to get out of a room.

It was what made her life easy, enabled her to bear her own pity.

She was walking back from the store with an eggplant, (the blind man had, after an elaborate pretence at weighing the plump vegetable, handed it to her wrapped in wax paper) keeping to the sides of the street, right up against the supports of billboards. She was not always able to manage it, but she liked to keep out of passing cars' lines of sight. She stood, cold, on a corner listening to the throaty disappearing of an engine, crossed the street. She passed two-story apartment buildings so plain as to reinforce the healing benefits of the rectangle in the minds of the occupants. In all she was inconspicuous, a smallish young woman carrying her canta. Now she vanished around a corner open to rows of more apartments. She began to pad for her keys in her large pocket. Four months she had lived with her love Kemal already before her marriage and she had three more to go, Kemal and his bossy mother and his slovenly brother Sa'im, Kemal no good to her at all, why the man was in the last stages of an illness with his studying for exams, when she spoke to him the many sheets of paper he had to lay aside before he listened were like so many bedclothes.

He stood directly across from the block and its tiny wrought-iron facing when Ayesha entered. He was leaning against a mailbox: he had found this to be his best method. In time the uncomfortable grate of arm against edge and the tapped feeling of all one's weight in one leg guaranteed a profile of such discomfort that it was effectively anonymous. He could wait and see which light came on, but he was virtually certain this was her, the sister. Or he could walk around the back. No, he could do that tomorrow. He was in no hurry and stayed leaning there a further twenty minutes. He watched his breath but it did not stop the ditty he'd heard on television from chasing its something-about-a-razor tail around in his head. From time to time he touched his upper lip with his sheathed fingers.

The first thing Ayesha did was to go to the kitchen table, pick up a match, strike the match and light the oil lamp, shake the match and watch the smoke tumble thin and up. Then there were the small pleasures of seeing the flame shape in the blue glass and the inner flame repeated, softer blue, signal flame, in the black windowpane. Then she got to work. She tossed a rag on the table and wiped it. She sliced and salted the eggplants good and long, had onions fried until a slick sweat formed on the eggplants and a rusting-apple brown blush began, and put them in the water, flame up, heavy lid down, peeled garlic, smelled her thumb. She looked forward to three hours from now, when she'd done her last dish and could walk over to Kemal where he was studying and lay her hands on his shoulders, then go do what she wanted. She cleaned up the living room. Sa'im came in. She was back in the kitchen making a mess of the board chopping tomatoes. Hauled up the pot and scraped into it, the red mess plopped and stuck to the sides, so she elbowed it down with her spoon.

Once Sa'im had watched her respond to three or four commands his mother had shot at her, and when the mother had left he asked her how she could stand it.

"I can stand it," she said. "There are other places to be."

"But you are here!"

"Evidently," she said.

Privately she wondered if there was something funny about the brother. He wasn't around that much. Ayesha would have loved to know what he did all day in that photo shop of his.

Privately Sa'im wondered if Kemal had gone mad and had hypothesized a strategic hibernation of the Ottomans—they had quietly slipped away and let the abolition of the Caliphate stand as a sort of alibi for their whereabouts, and in their smoking jackets continued to be absent, sleeping directly through this nation-state period, patiently teaching their children (to hand to them) customs administrative, financial, bureaucratic, tax-pivotal, semi-tribal, providing their heirs with all the moral fortitudes and loadings of an essentially Eurocentric leisure class military clique, complete with computerized chessboards. While the Empire lay silently breeding, on another level it grossly burgeoned, a vast shadow network of unregistered import-export companies, all done with wartime land-transport and foreign freighters badly needing repair, of soccer-spinoff publishing ventures and small monopolies on building materials. Ottoman children forbidden to take their Arabic books and writing materials out of the house. How do you know they exist? These are the people who always go to the mosque and you don't know them because you never go.

Sa'im imagined Kemal working all this out in his binders, taping newspaper clippings onto foolscap, he would get to the bottom of these imaginary Ottomans and then forget it. A whole negative register, an understory, entirely plausible complete with captions. Lost, gone. Kemal does not have the imagination to see it, he thought.

The idea would intrigue and then amuse Sa'im for a few days. When snapping his portrait-officers he would catch himself grinning, having mentally stripped and refitted that bored and serious young face as an Ottoman spy, pushing out the moustache and adding fez. Emboldened by his silent hilarity, he would forget himself and rush forward to push his subject's head to the left or right, whichever fleshed out his fantasy better.

They sat around the kitchen table after dinner. Kemal asked

him how many schools were constructed during the Tanzimat. Sa'im in turn asked him to compare defence expenses from the mid-fifties to the present in light of NATO commitments. A sifting into of time phases took place; each savoured the expected silence, tension, the resumption of silence. Mother switched off her radio and sang half a song, then switched it on again. Ayesha got up and collected glasses, started to make a new pot of tea. Mother sang again. Ayesha came and stood behind Kemal, put her hands on his shoulders. "Nato is overcommitted," Mother said. Only Ayesha turned to look at her.

Halima, she-who-made-pharmaceuticals, the girl he had been seeing, had a permanent measure of penitence in her eyes, as though next-to-do was always that which she'd feel sorry for. Too, when they met in secret she was always silent for a long moment and always stood in the middle of the studio and unpinned and took her hair down, letting her hands enter her hair and push up near the nape, disappear, and merge, stretching fingers and arms, the hair finely falling as she stretched her whole back and legs on her tiptoes and Sa'im liked that, ached, to be honest, for it and could never think of anything to say when she had finished and turned to him.

They went into Sa'im's darkroom, where they at least knew each other and had been before. Outside, in the evident clarity of the office whether grappling, or trying to talk, or uneasy over the desk, things were less and less familiar than here where the dimmest of red lighting glowed and things could be confusing, yes, but never dangerous. They sighted slowly and spoke in the dark. Faintly, away on the street below, they could hear other people talking.
    "This, it must be a draft or something," Sa'im said. "There is a hole."

Entire quarter-hour efforts would sustain a waterlogged conversation, during which he found it increasingly desirable and difficult to touch her, and Halima's face would shift, lose, like a lifted film, its prettiness and reveal the older woman living in her with scruples and worries and the skittish flicker in her eyes, surprisingly dull. The pains began in his stomach, knits, then knots.

His hand kept changing and changing the stations of the radio, fuzzing into fussing into fuzz.

"Give me a kiss."
    She tried to push at his tongue with hers: misinterpreted.
    "I will show you orgasm!"
    She stiffened, and pushed him away.

They listened to the traffic.

"You are so handsome, not like me."
    "No, I am humanist."
    "I am ashamed for my family's sake."
    "Why are you crying?" he said.
    "You will leave me."

She slid away in a cab at Sultanahmet Square and he bought a bottle of Raki and some Maltepes, and walked back to the office.
    He walks into his office, and he is reading a letter over and over.
    He shuffled the pages and began again; the horrible feeling started much sooner this time, made him pinch his eyes. He placed the letter on his desk and lit a cigarette.
    He lights a cigarette.
    Dear Sa'im:
    He had found the letter halfway up the stairs, as usual. He noticed again the chain hanging from the shattered lightbulb, and vowed he would fix that. He was repelled, but read one phrase: *this is not the life together I had imagined for us.*
    Like a direct communication from another planet: alien and theatrical. *The life together.* Alan's blue summer suit, and camera strap; he never took the camera off, even while eating. A dinner in Sultanahmet, more of a visit to the pub. Burgers and fries. They had talked for hours, played cards. He had kept lending coins to Alan so he could get toilet paper for the washroom. He loved the silliest drinks: bright green nane, the sweet scent detectable across the table. He remembered his own voice: "Yes, I'll see many girls there, in Scotland, I hope." Alan had laughed. Had he? "I bet you will, for a while."
    He got up, walked once around the room. *I am looking for evidence*, he thought, and laughed high, silly-fatigue.
    He looks for evidence, then.

He was standing with the big Redhouse dictionary in his hand. "For Sa'im, may this open up your intellect and feelings." This in English, of course.

He sat down again with the book on his lap.

I imagined for us.

And this was the part Sa'im just didn't get: Alan, by himself, imagining it, this wonderful life he was going to have with him. Alan must have taken certain steps already, financial, perhaps he had written other letters, arranged something, rented something. He must have jotted down a few notes to himself sitting up in a motel bed in Northern Scotland. He had promised Sa'im a job selling photographic equipment and a relatively cheap work permit.

He goes out for some tea then.

He locked the door, he walked back and forth outside.

Late afternoon, the heat not coming on, ever, unless he got up and did something, he read that his silence "*was too much to bear*," and that "*It hurts...as directly as I have, or dare, I must...*", the heat never coming, darker, dimmer.

On the street a child called out once, for *Balid, Balid*.

Sa'im just stood there, yards and yards from this crowd who were waving big signs and placards, and let the booming booming words of the distant megaphone reach him. It was coming from a large, high stage at the other end of the square. Skies very grey. High up, above them, hanging, silent (drowned) was the *Iyigünler* helicopter, washing, washing the rain down into the square. Heads moved up and down. Sa'im got more into the shelter of the buildings, moving sideways, his hands in his pockets. A man among men—which?—was yelling, very loudly, very slowly, about things that would not stop, would not be tolerated, would not do you Turkish people any good. There were over a million Turks in Transania. Some of them had been forced to take Transanian surnames, and they were not permitted to speak, or teach, the Turkish language. Sa'im knew about all this. But what would the demonstration accomplish? He tried to remember what sort of immigration agreements there were between the Transanian government and his (ha), but couldn't. They would be very poor, these other Turks. Do we really want them here? He was trifly shamed to be thinking this when so many ranked in front of him were so heatedly concerned. There had been riots. There had been beatings. There had been women and children tampered with, violated, when husbands were off working in other Transanian cities. The crowd kept getting bigger and bigger. Few wanted to miss getting wet in the square, because it was almost certainly going to rain harder, and everyone would be soaked, and then, maybe, they would be less angry, but then again, maybe they would be angrier. He watched the row of backs for sudden movements, raised arms, swiftly drawn-back legs. There were none. He felt relatively safe there under the building's awning—he turned, stepped back, and saw it was the Tütünbank—and brightening some, actually said hello to some of the bank people who had come out of the building, on their lunch hour or something, to see what was happening in the square, and join in, at the back of the crowd, with their open coats and their paper bags or wax paper bundles they munched from. Sa'im admired the hair and bearing of the women. And how was he to get the money to Halima? The speaker at the front went on: our people, friends, taxed, burdened, bludgeoned, denied, raped of their status, cuckolded (the crowd stamped! shouted!) defrauded, undernourished, set upon, educated to be unTurkish!, silenced in their own tongue! our people under another government bullied, beaten, bashed, allowed only the rudiments of recognition (all swelled, fomenting in the spit of their own pain), forbidden to practise their religion, their customs, our customs, arise! And they did, lifting as much as they could with their shoes still on the wet ground, chanting, declaiming, following the rhythm suggested by the speaker's frantic, hopping dance. Sa'im wondered how long this would have to go on before he felt involved.

He heard vans pulling up, the blast of doors, to his left, and right, doors slamming on the other side of the square; he was not surprised to see police stepping out, standing silently at the edges, or slowly walking outside the shoving, changing mass. Police stopped again, scanning, looking at faces, holding their riot sticks against their buttons, eyes purposely set and blank. Somone brushed Sa'im.

He jumped, and slipped away.

He got two blocks and he could hear the crowd, the announcing noise, he walked faster, then one or two came pounding up behind him, running hard, their faces wholly set on escape, then one or two more, and he started to run, and as he did he heard a whole riverbank of people turning a corner, the police not far behind, but why, what was the matter with the protest, what was going on? He ran more deliberately, slowing to a pace he could sustain if he had to, then he swerved and followed a man in a green cap into a building up one flight of stairs, and the man sat on the landing and watched him come up, his eyes wide with fear as Sa'im hauled himself up the last few stairs by the bannister.

"Not me," he said.

"Do not be stupid. I am not the police."

"Not me."

Sa'im sat down beside him.

A siren, winding and winding in the streets.

"Don't you do anything to me," the man said.

"Relax. Here, have a cigarette."

But the man could not bear it any longer, he hurried up, pushing Sa'im down, and fled down the stairs. Silently, Sa'im crept to the entrance, after waiting to make sure the man was well outside the building. It seemed very quiet on the streets. He hunched against the doorjamb, the door an inch open; he couldn't see anything moving. He was out of breath. Nothing had happened.

This Hawkshi sheikh, who had been giving *khutba* upstairs since Ozgen's death, turned out to be the most aware individual Sa'im had ever seen. His manner, though calm, indeed he often spoke with his fingers interlocked on his belly, was devoted to monitoring, a comprehensive, clear scrutiny of all who passed in front of him, or wished to speak with him, and those movements and gestures behind the folding chairs at the limits of the room, much of which his audience was not aware of, and he continued this practise so there seemed an almost palpable presence directly before him, an additive organism of assembling information. Meanwhile he spoke, intending always the epigrammatic, or the story so pointless, so oblique, that it escaped the attention and floated above Hawkshi's head, a serene painted carpet of anecdotal characters ready for reference. Hawkshi said nothing specific, framed everything slightly away from those who listened and therefore had to move. His Arabic was beautiful. It called so little attention to itself when he mounted the *minbar* and began to give *khutba*, but the consonants were so effortless and flawlessly edged to a veracious and unexagerrated depth of emphasis that one listened as if under a continuous green breaking wave of the etched-in language.

Sa'im had heard of Hawkshi. The itinerant. Before he had been in Syria, had escaped Hama, walking out, so he had heard.

Then Sudan. Egypt. He was nearly assassinated at an airport in Canada. These scenes assembled around Hawkshi like panels. But what was he doing within them?

One evening Sa'im sat at his desk, deliberating on possible Alan-responses when the door opened and Sheikh Hawkshi entered. He was in his familiar jellaba. Sa'im realized he had probably come down after *'Isha* prayers.

They sat.

Hawkshi used a lot of *kohl*.

"Can you do 12 passport-size of me for starters. I'll pay you generously, *insha'Allah*."

He tapped on the desk.

They did it. Hawkshi had a nervous smile at the flash, but his imperturbable fingers twiddled on. A week later he was back; he tossed a wide manila envelope on the desk in front of Sa'im, who looked up from his raki and a magazine.

"I need these in two days," he said, "The names are on the negative strips, and you can, if it isn't too much trouble,——"he produced a wad of bills, "insert and affix the photographs to the passports. And thank you."

Sa'im sat up straight and snapped the bills. Hawkshi was gone.

Crossing Sultanahmet Square Sa'im heard a voice call his name. He turned full circle. Then he saw it was Khazar in a flimsy shirt sweeping off his uncle's steps. Sa'im waved.

Kemal held the door open for her and Ayesha entered and they walked down the steps, arm in arm, into the Café Platin. They had gone here often when Kemal had started studying, she liked the cafe, she liked the man in his sweater who nodded then behind his table with the change box and his two packs of cigarettes open in front of him, barking at the waiters who were slim and attentive. She liked the smell of the place, tea and smoke, recent steam. She liked the red velvet paint and the gold brocade on the walls and the big painting of Ataturk at the far end; how she liked the young men in the military and the way they crossed their legs under their heavy coats at the many round tables and she liked the smoothness of their faces as they had shaved before coming. Voices of the women too in the Café Platin, and the cards and chips all over the tables and the chatter: hurried, captious, so loud you never heard your spoon in your tea tinkle. She walked in a fog of her own

90

contentment as she tried to find them a table, something Kemal wasn't very good at. He was always asking if tables were empty that were obviously occupied. She found one, finally, but then that would happen anyway, she liked just walking around in the confusion, the happiness—the Café Platin made her feel happy. And there was music playing, music of all these cardplayers gathered to hear it. She slipped her coat off and smoothed the edges of her *hejab*.

"You know you can take that off, you know."

"I think I will keep it on."

Kemal looked about for a waiter.

He looked up, blinking, from the letter on his desk, woozy and unaware of how long he had sat. He decided to slip out for something to eat, and left the letter open on the desk.

The next morning it was gone. Sa'im, at first, had skirted Sultanahmet and took a long, steep street to the west. He stood in the middle of the street and could make out the relief of bricks in the lamplight around Marmara University, spilling inward from the Hippodrome. There were silhouettes and breathclouds coming from the corner baklavacesi. He could go to the Hürriya, or turned up the steep street to the west, which hooked around a dark doored corner about thirty shining wet bricks away. Sa'im heard the water running in the gutters and walked against its noise. It was just dark so a face approaching became a face in a film walking past, that light in which letters of storesigns seem to drop forever. He stood looking downhill towards Kennedy Caddesi and the water. Here there was an iron fence lit all around a public building. He kept walking, not hungry at all, keyed up. He paid longer attention to the conversations he heard as he passed people; he never went down here. He didn't know anybody. A car, blaring, blaring, passed him. A cat jumped out of a doorway, it skittered about, went black.

He did go into a pide shop and had cheese pide and ayram, chewed and drank without tasting much.

He didn't know this area at all. He turned North, towards Divan Yolu. He was there in a few minutes. A taxi hissed past. Should he go home?

A car cutting out of the dark blaaared him back to the curb, he watched it pass, and hailed the group walking over to him. "Hey, where is this?"

"Aw, this is Hayratamasay. Where are you going?"

"I don't know."

They looked each other up and down.

"I'm just walking. Suleymaniye maybe."

"Aw, Suleymaniye you're way past."

"Yes, I know. Thank you."

"You want Suleymaniye? Why?"

Sa'im blinked at him.

"You know someone in Suleymaniye?"

Two of them looking down the street, over their shoulders, and back at him. Then the one of them that hadn't said anything yet stepped up and said, "Don't you know, bébé?"

Sa'im just walked away from them. He got to the end of the street, looked back, there were four of them when there were only three. He had never heard of Hayratamasay. He walked quicker, listened for the water, heard traffic, evidently pitched through many buildings, it was no help.

Stopped dead in the middle of the street. For a moment brought his hands to his ears, rubbed them, warmed them.

And lit another cigarette, and began to walk again.

If he could have known that he wouldn't have wanted to have Alan think that he would or would not he would have taken him up on it. No.

Took a deep drag. He came to a viaduct underpass, peeked in and sloshed through an inch of water over matting newspapers bright and lined at his feet. He slogged and sloshed through to the end, and came out in a yard whose whole extent and contour was a puddle, more like a shallow lake with gravel underneath. And over the whole yard a fine mist, a tight upstitching but infinitesimal rain. There were lights affixed to outbuildings—they looked like auto-repair sheds, the flat triangular valences of the lights over the doorframes, big black doors, rusty low sheds, colours unclear. There were yellow machines parked on the stones on the other side of the lake. A depot. He recognized an asphalt roller; it had a cab on it, the door hanging open.

He found his coat too tight to play with the gears and the levers, so he loosened it, looking around to get a better sense of barking somewhere, beyond the overpass, tied in the courtyard of a thin glow he saw high in the air. The cars were in that direction too; only they sounded, as he moved the shift in the gear box back and up into third, and pressed in the clutch, they sounded blinder and blinder, as if they were creeping slowly through the city around the yard.

A clicking action.

A voice behind him said, "Get down, hands up. Get out of the cab. Do it."

He did. His coat got caught in the door, and he had to free it; the man's feet shifted on the gravel. Sa'im stepped down backwards, into four inches of water, peripherally aware of his shape. He thought he had a dog with him, but the dog wasn't doing anything but breathing. It was his own breathing.

"Hands straight up."

He felt the rain on his fingertips high above his head.

"I could shoot you. Who are you? What are you doing on my machine?

"I could shoot you, who the fuck are you?

"Come here.

"Don't move."

His steps came up behind Sa'im.

"Turn around."

The man wore a hooded raincoat. There was a dog. There was a shotgun. The man held it like he was poling a door in, made a jab, at Sa'im's stomach. He was breathing hard.

"I meant no harm."

"Shut up!"

"Yes."

"Walk over to the viaduct," the man said at length.

Sa'im turned stiffly and walked to the entrance.

"In it."

He went about ten yards in.

"Get on your knees."

He did, on his hands, then knees.

"You are crazy!" Sa'im screamed.

The shotgun went off, boom, BOOM, again out of the tunnel far behind him. Sa'im ran, knowing the first shot had been in the air, to scare him, he jumped over a can, but he wasn't too sure about the second, and he heard steps behind him steps with claws in them, he turned and tripped and rolled and got up running along a darker street and the dog was on him, bit painfully into his leg and he got it by the throat and it on its back clawed at his face and he smashed, smashed, smashed the dog's head on the wet street until it was dead and the dog changed into a man with rain in his mouth, and Sa'im walked up to a parked car and sat on the hood.

Who knows, he might be quite near Zeyrek.

93

Around the next corner he broke out of the streetmaze and stood at the edge of a broad avenue overlooking the Halic. Fresher air. He was not near Zeyrek at all. The reflection of the great mosque hung inverted in the waters, as he made his way, doing his coat snug again, up its steps and into great doors. No one was inside. The chandeliers burned brightly into the mihrabs in the walls, finding each one, and lit as tenuously as upward as they could the enlettered shields but never finding the utmost touch of the dome in the air.

When he went outside he was unsurprised to see another man waiting for him at the bottom of the stairs, hands cupped around a cigarette, and it was to Sa'im that he offered this cigarette at the bottom of the stairs. Sa'im took it, and the man, having accomplished something, lit another one and stepped away.

"I must be going," said Sa'im.

"Oh, come on."

"I want to get out of the rain.Thank you, goodbye."

But the man was keeping pace with him. "What a funny man you are, who are you? What are you doing out here and all alone."

Sa'im sensed an inclining directness to the question, and he ignored it. The ferries were docked at Eminönü. When he reached them, he would turn around and come back to the mosque, and he would leave, lose, if necessary, this man.

"What are you doing?"

"I am walking and you are following me."

"But what is the purpose of your activity?"

"You want to find out something about me. But there is nothing—yok."

"You are too modest. There was plenty to find out about you."

Sa'im got to the gate, and turned. In the little arch of the door, way, way away, he saw the shape of the man in his coat, small-small, all the turalar leaning to the lane. There was a lightning-flash and at the end of the lane with the leaning turalar, a man-shape in a coat, and Sa'im heard him laugh, tiny, in the other gate-door, a man laughing in a dark wet arch, away, the wind whipped over the lettered faces of the turalar and through the branches. Saw him laughing at him, though far away, a figure in a coat open like a door.

Sa'im didn't sleep that night. He was being followed. The only person Sa'im knew who had been followed had also been in jail for two years; he had returned to Istanbul, and waved, today, at Sa'im across Sultanahmet square. He was thin, crazed, sweeping off the steps of his uncle's shop. This boy spent a lot of time at the Hürriya where he told tourists about his prison term, got them to write love letters to foreign girls he had met. Although he became better at tavla and at making near-meaningful conversation at the bar he was unable to shake that crazed look in his eyes, nor do more than sweep off his uncle's steps; he had merged with his imprisonment.

He went to the Hürriya. He had to roust a woman from her bed in the basement to open the doors. "Where is your brother?" he asked her.

At first she wouldn't tell him.

"He is gone?"

"Yes, he went to Germany. "

"I am sorry to wake you up. Where is Emin?"

"He is up in the bar."

And she lay her cheek in her hand, and closed her lids.

Emin was awake, though, dancing and dancing around the tables with the stupidest look on his face, with a mad, loud, folk song in the blaster. Sa'im checked—no one was there—and went behind the bar, switched it off.

"Emin."

"Fuck off, my music!"

"Emin come here, I want to talk."

He made a loud grumbling sound, and kicked over a table. Then, his eyes red, hair fuming from his sweaty head, he strode up to the bar and swept glasses into the sidesink with a crash and glared at Sa'im. He banged one then another bottle on the bar.

"We will drink!"

"No."

"Then I will drink!"

"You know some of the police, don't you?"

"They are a bunch of criminals. Yes, a few."

"I need you to talk to them."

Emin poured whiskey all over the bar and slurped it up with his lips.

"Come, have a drink."

Emin found two glasses, which he filled.

"Rifat, he tells me how to run this, run that, fuck off Rifat, I

95

will run the bar, I will mind my own business, fuck you Rifat alçak."

And he took a big drink and said, "What do you want the police for?"

"They are following me."

"They follow everybody, they are a bunch of thugs. They will not talk to you."

"They'll talk to you."

"What are they? I know one or two, they fill out forms." His eyes clouded, trying to picture them; he shrugged and took an even bigger drink from his glass."I would like to help you, but."

"Tell them to stop following me."

"But there are a lot of things I can do nothing about. Many things, many things..."

"They'll hurt me," Sa'im said.

"But Sa'im, Sa'im, what are they following you for, the police? Hmm? And what can I do?"

"You said you see them and you get what's her——Kathy's visa like extended."

"Kathy? Bad, bad, very bad."

"Emin, this is a problem here."

"Is not such a big problem."

Emin poured another large drink.

"But I cannot those. For they will not. And I do not. But I have a big problem. It is Kathy."

"Emin, the police! What about Kathy?"

"I love her but she loves another." His lips and eyes were about the same colour: gassed embarrassments.

Sa'im knew then he had to get out of there.

"I love Kathy but she loves another!"

He went home.

In other parts of the country they had been detained, a great number of them. There were a few photos of the captured, men and women, having been asked to stand in rows in front of a long table on which were piled bundles of weapons and explosives. On the TV screen it looked like a lysesi gymnasium. They were Kurds, Armenians, students, peace supporters, housewives, professors, country doctors.

Their activities were unrepublican.

The first thing he noticed was the missing letter. He ran around the tiny office, checking other things. He swore, and hit the desk. He made a phone call. "Where are the pamphlets?"

"Sa'im?"

"Yes, it's me. Did you take them?"

"What? Which?"

"The pamphlets—you gave them to me."

"Oh those. Just a second here. Got to. Okay, they were for another group. We traded off."

Sa'im was silent. Then he said,

"What were they about?"

"Chemical weapons mostly. Types of genocide. A human rights group. What's up? Did you want some more?"

In the huge halled mirrored and chandeliered and braziered but hanging cold, golden-floored other country of the Dolmabahçe Palace there is another group going through: Americans, Germans, Russians, Canadians, Yugoslavians, French, Italians, Swedes, Finns, English, it is a large group. They are all tall and wear raincoats. They come from the North and the West, from the districts of Marlborough, Blaupunkt, Stolichkya, Chanel, Boda, Dijon and Vuarney, Chianti, Bols and Bors, Dunhill and Savile. They carry Japanese cameras.

He is going through the palace with them, very slow.

They turn and admire, admire and turn, clinging to each other in tall clusters.

He flips his beads, he flips his beads.

They are a wandering node of objective historical consciousness, he thinks. They are the pillars of industrial consumption, he thinks. They are post-imperialist amnesiacs, big tippers.

He leads them through the Pasha's room.

"Rococco," someone says, "what a word."

A table, a chair, a television monitor. As they point happily at the woodwork, he pays attention to the screen. On Iyigünler there is an interview with the President; in his full-cheeked manner he is telling the people, represented by a woman with big shoulderpads on, that he feels confident. In what, she asks? In the Turkish people.

The guide's eyes narrow. He flips his beads.

Sa'im was still sitting with the phone in his hands when Hawkshi barged into the office. Hawkshi asked bluntly, "What kind of matte are you using? "

"Pardon?"

"The finish. Our stamp is smearing. We have to make a correction."

"I don't have any other paper," Sa'im said.

"Then get some." He thrust a great deal of money at Sa'im. He bent to warm his hands at the heater. "Now."

Sa'im dropped to his knees as the light went on and the lines and lines of miniature eager policemen, caught, with their badges and hands in their laps and hats, in the instant their fear-making in him became human, that is to say the past. They were still there, rows in red light. He checked the trays in which a few more passportees were floating, face up, lividly and gently rocking. He stood up, marvelling. He had made a cave of faces.

He crowded with the others after the soup outside the restaurant in the shadow of their bus, which reared out of the ground shining with frost. They were outside a kitchen-shop with pots and pans and packages of noodles; he was blankly looking at these through metal slit-slats when someone produced a set of pipes and a circle formed, and the men began singing, round and round in their side-stepping ring, and every time Sa'im came around with them the mongoloid boy said *Tekerlek* in his scaly voice. They were very loud, it was freezing. They danced and the player played.

You can get off the wheel now.

Tekerlek, went the boy.

Under the dim lights high in the dome, where a picture, a framed oil of the leader is vast and static, conveying an aura of celestial event in the cigarette smoke, among the crowd the man is sending a package from Sirkeçi Postane. Hundreds cross the marble floor in leisurely rapid patterns, as in a railway station, absorbing the back and forth barks of transactions and the blast and thump of seals and stamps without a blink. It takes him ages to reach the door. He is back, approximately, to where he started from this morning. He quickly leaves these streets, and walks out alone on Sarayburnu headland, the lower road skirting the edges of the Halic shore. Strong wind, weeds and dark, wet trees waver up the clay faces of the cliffs.

He lifts his feet through the grasses of the verge. Endlessly his eyes range, colorless, inhabited. Endlessly he places one foot ahead of the other. Then, in the twilight ahead, three figures gain shape, shift and shortnesses over the ground. A man, a woman fully robed, a child. The man is shouldering a basketload of coal.

They pay no attention to him, and his shoulders barely swivel as they pass around his back. They work on in the darkness, in encroaching folds.

The man is visible for a moment or two longer. He is hunkering, blowing on his hands.

And out of the strict and distant pilings in this new and luminous night with its displaced hint of chemical violet a distant engine is huffing, chuffs. A periscope and turret bulk in the middle distance, clearly numbered, the chop wetting the numbers, covering them, it begins to slide beneath. Two birds lift from the silhouette, the turning eyestem sinking down to an anonymous face, beneath the waters. Again the muezzin: *ALLAHU AKBAR ALLAHU AKBAR.* The submarine cruises just above the water's surface, a black kerchief but lightly disturbed by the city windows, or the odd set of running lights. *LA ILAHA ILLA ALLAH.*

Wind. The sound of grasses.

His heart grew light in the waters.

The Mill

The Dryers

Yesterday I was over at Jeff's and I

started thinking about the mill again. We were vegging out in the living room. He told me that Tabby McMack was back working on the spreaders.

"He was a total washout as a foreman," I said.

"Well, spreaders, least he knows how to do that. Foreman, he had no clue. From what I hear that new super what's-his-name is kicking some ass down there."

I am nobody in particular. My people aren't either, only semi-successfully transplanted. I went through a loathing of things Anglo-Saxon and said once—driving through Oak Bay past an upscale jeep—that they were essentially frightened of machinery; the reason they took to gardening was, being inept and frightened, their spades, stuck in the ground leaned on, hobbled over, kept them from falling down. I (their son) got a degree in something that didn't interest me, another in one that did, but wreaked no employment out of either training. I was given to leisurely pranks, tomfoolery with cohorts, general incompatibility with paid exertion. I worked in a court. I did drugs. I taught: badly. Eventually, through more drugs, and due to my idle habits of intellectual speculation, drifting downwards, I came to work at the mill. Not to put too bleak a face on it, but at the time I recognized that, though this was employment, I was nearing the bottom. When I was younger I heard much talk of the fall of capitalism. Now I was walking around unprotected from its falling shards.

Number two dryer was the first machine I saw at the mill. Two cardboard signs were taped where the feeder couldn't avoid seeing them:

LOOK BEFORE THROWING VENEER BEHIND YOU.

And,

NO. 4—NO FEEDIE.

I was famous for late breaks when I did clean-up. I would take my last break on the night shift a little after midnight. As I drank my coffee the graveyard shift was coming in. Exhausted, I'd walk back into the mill and collect the brooms. I remember absently listening to all the noises as I did this and suddenly being aware of another, rarer zone of noise, an alluring vibration so enmeshed in the other sounds it was a siren. I stopped and listened harder with a broom in each hand. Then I walked, drawn, over near the dryers. The eerie pinging tribulations that sounded so much like a Chinese piece of music, atonal in a disorienting, distorting way, turned out to be the music of the dryers cooling. Jig had the big doors open at the side and the yards and yards of dryer-trays were drying, unwarping, singing in this strange, elevated way.

Jig walked from door to door and played his flashlight over the rows and rows of toothed dark rotors to make sure each of them was turning.

The Spreaders

Bill was going to take a trip. I caught up to him the parking lot that Friday after the last leg of the shift had been a disaster. I had been laying, beating the press, just zipping along when I looked up and the rollers were white. Whizzing bone dry. The whole load was dry. There wasn't any glue in the spreader at all when we stopped and checked. Jackson turned from what he was doing on the press to laugh at us (we had to take the whole load apart and toss out the core, which got marginally darker with glue by the bottom of the load). And then spreader number two had gone and done the same thing about an hour later, just before quitting time.

"So where you going on your trip, Bill."

"Brazil."

"No." I was imagining sepia stigmata of underdevelopment: underprivileged louts in villages hiking into the big cities, drugged up, yelping as in a documentary on the tops of trains, ready to pimp and loot. As of smooth dictators in decky uniforms. The unnamed alleys where the disappeared were to be found. "Oh yeah, why there?"

"I hear it's a real party place, man, just beach and parties and gentle hippy type loving people," said Bill. "We wanna surf when we get there."

We stood around then in the parking lot, slightly or really giddy, when of a sudden we could see, then hear a van moving through the parking lot and stopped a hundred yards from us. The foreman's exaggeratedly patient polite voice came floating toward us. "Is Wigan there? Wigan? I want to speak to him. "

He knew damn well Wigan was; otherwise he would never have stopped. He would have sailed out of the parking lot towards Admirals at great speed, swerved and missed the pothole.

Wigan muttered *fuck* and started to walk towards the van.

102

"He's gonna give us shit," said Jackson with real regret. "Fuck."

"Well, go on," said Chambers, "you better go and help him out."

"No fucking way. I've been drinking. He'll think I've been drinking all night."

We couldn't hear the foreman and Wigan talking over the motor and Chamber's throbbing new car. I winced over at it because a ballad was beginning, like a sappy lake in the middle of the thrash.

Bill and Chambers exchanged thumbs-ups.

"It's a sweet song," Bill sighed.

Wigan was hunched at the driver's window, one hand on the mirror. He looked mostly at the ground, his spine curled that way too, in humpy dejection, a deformity oddly noticeable at a distance in such a forceful, kinetic man. Yet even from there it was possible to see his quasimo stiffen and shake. Then we heard them.

"We're all gonna get shit," said Jackson and shook out a cigarette and lit it squinting.

Chambers sucked on his beer and cluck-clucked his face.

Wigan came marching back among us, swinging his beer can. Before anyone could ask him he started talking. "I told him he was being an asshole, calling me over and chewing me out in front of my friends. You're playing a real power thing, Tabby, I says and he says, 'Hell no, hey buddy , if I get shit you get shit, I gotta give you shit.' 'Fine,' I says, 'I'll come in early Monday and we'll both get shit together, let's get this thing right out in the open.'"

Wigan stopped and tapped his foot, then said,"That fucking guy really bugs me, the way he's always weaseling around trying to get that extra eight ten per cent out of you when you're already giving a hundred. No——I mean it. We don't fuck around on the spreaders, we fucking go at it."

There was a chorus of confirmation, concluded by one of Jackson's patented *fucking rights*.

Smith, owly eyed, his legs crossed on a log, said seriously, "It's hard work."

Wigan was the only one I ever heard telling Tabby how hard he thought we worked. He used it as a blunt thrust, the opening round of his evening's jousts with Tabby. "Let me tell you something. I haven't stopped sweating since I walked through that door." But among the crews there was silence about the pace of the job, nothing public was said about fatigue. Once I heard Ned, my sheet turning partner (who I know often had little sleep because of his colicky baby) say, at the last break on a rainy night shift, "It's hard to keep up that pace," to Jackson. They had been turning sheets on one for six hours with full sheet core. Jackson had simply acknowledged the statement and stared into his coffee, replied with a stoic undertone, "Yeah, it's tough," the selfsame way he said, "Shit happens". But his face was white, had a sweat sheen. He was sucking air.

With the notable exception of Calum, whose response to all pressure was to go around chatting, anything to slow us down, bargaining for his own brand of lackadaisicality, the spreader crews worked flat out, and as we worked, kept up a constant banter. Essentially we were having a couch party interrupted by the mere trivialities of thudding sheets and blasting arms, and of the turning, beautifully puffed and bowed sheets that relaxed to the table over the ducking, catching, adjusting, spinning, stripping and ducking core layer, the core streaming from the rollers across the browning bed.

There was a code of speed. Slowness was resented, mocked. Once you got used to the spreaders at a competitive pace there was no slowing down, it was unthinkable because time dragged like a dusty toffee when you did. Often, turning on one, when a slow forklift driver was driving for us and we had to stop, and wait around for new core, new backs, where the fuck is the guy, HEY, an almost unbearable irritation built up in the arms, and in the mornings it was accompanied by a murderous resentment of the cold. We stood rubbing our arms and swearing sporadically into the din. It was like being woken up every twenty minutes or so on night duty at a psychiatric ward to deal with violent head-wound patients. We throbbed. When the core came we nearly shoved it through the side of the litter box we had wanted to jam it in, if possible kill the core feeder. Which was whimpering Calum.

He lifted up the top core to show us something poor him just couldn't begin to deal with and when we didn't respond he shouted, "It's him, slow, eh. I—what can I do, I got to throw this junk away."

"Just feed the fucking core."

"Sure, just like Stubby."

Jackson was always nodding at Calum when he wasn't looking and saying softly, *What a dipshit.*

"I got to work fast. It's the only way to go." Chambers lay as he explained." Right now we're going like this, I'm not even thinking about my job, I'm thinking what video should I rent tonight, did I leave the stove on. When you're going fast, you only think about your job, you're not over there Smith is sitting down why can't I do that. You're just thinking job."

You could never talk anyone out of anything at the mill. Disagreement was fundamentally taboo. People from time to time made announcements, outright challenges in the lunchroom and it was expected that their pronouncements would be endorsed. Otherwise there was little point in saying anything. There was respect, though sometimes only respectful silence, for even the stupidest plans put forward, the most incorrect assessments, the pettiest accusations. I fell into this too. It became such a bother to genuinely disagree, and you could tell, the other guy would immediately change modes and talk about something else or go through a little act where he can't believe you disagree with him, then restate his case. Me. Wurn. Jeff and Jackson and Smith and Floyd. Calum. Süleyman. Nasiir. Chambers and Wigan. Every single last one of us was right.
There were exceptions.

Aspirophors I discovered were those incandescently tense situations when someone decides to make an event other than, usually greater than, what it was intended to be—as when, say, a visiting poet shows up at a casual dinner before a reading and proceeds to insist on lecturing the other eaters the whole time on dialectics, using often the words "elite groups", "paradigm" and "Kuwait." There were also bathetophors: occasions of collapsing purpose, as when Tabby the foreman was yanked away from giving us hell by something more urgent but not yet clear to him. When called on, his face collapsed and became a worried cave of the what-do-I-do-now variety, and off he ran.
There were also pantophors, when the virus of communication came over someone in their arms and legs and they acted out some simple plea for you, some instruction, Jig continuously taking keys from his pocket, from his beltloop, from a long dirty chain and explaining carefully the advantages of keeping your keys each way, with illustrative tugs and hefts. He kept producing more keys and examples of his keykeeping. Aspirophors. Bathetophors. Pantophors. The world was simple, labelled. The mind could go to sleep to turn some sheets.

105

Pathetophor: Tabby flared up and yelled,"Listen, if I get shit you get shit."

There was an entire philosophy in the schema. The cave I was in was finished, flowering with machine-mouths.

Dryers. Hot Patch. Sander.

Coffee.

Wurn, his hair blown back, hunched, his hand shooting out to hit the grader buttons, his head not moving at all—motionless except for his eyes, which I was intensely aware of (he had light blue eyes) after he mentioned they were tired. Front of panel, back, mirror, rear, front. His eyes forever jerked over the dimensions of each panel——rapid, intense action in a small space, every unblink absorbing ninety-six square feet of plywood surface and four edges of panel into his pupils. His gloves had holey fingers and he sipped a huge cardboard cup of Mac's coffee. I didn't like to think too much about Wurn up there, grading. It made me nervous, disturbed me. Locked and locked again, his eyes in their constricted play, the jabbing finger.

There was a huge sign on the office wall near where we punched in which compared our safety record with other co-operative mills. There were slots for accident frequency per year and number of accident free days this month. One of the older guys who got the soft job of office clean-up had to keep this sign up to date. Often we saw him standing in front of it scratching his head and wiping a big number 1 on his jeans leg. There were safety posters and reminders and signs and illustrations of untimely death all over the mill.

The Kid came over to the spreaders to get Wigan—with a spear nicely slivered into his inside elbow. The Kid was moving slowly, helping the elbow with his hand and balancing the sliver along his forearm. Wigan stopped feeding and ran down to him, and, palms down, pranced. "OK. Look. Wait right here. No. Get the forklift."

He ran off to do that, the Kid's face hanging there. Behind that gaping ache, the press platform clanked upward, across the slats of vivid steam. Smith and Mord rowing panels in. Behind the small press, the bell went off, and the red blinker on the track began to flash.

"Where the fuck is he," said the kid.

That was the Kid, speared with his sliver easily a foot long.

106

The tip bulged under his skin. The time Mahmood swung and spun a sheet of clear-face and caught me on the side of the helmet. Later a forklift would run over my foot. Someone on the other shift got their foot stuck under the press platform and above the edge of the floor—he was off for a while. Jackson's back got cranked by the arm which had, as we liked to put it, operated randomly and slammed down on him when he was patching an end, pinning him by the lower back to the bed. I saw Jack with the trick knee catch, alarmed, an upending hunk of core and grasp it with its sharp end an inch from his eye: his knee held. Smith had been hit smack in the forehead with a piece of core and I saw it.

NO JOB IS SO IMPORTANT THAT YOU CAN'T TAKE THE TIME TO GET INJURED ON IT.

He bled in an half-inch stitch at the top of his nose. A steam pipe, heating merrily mainly thin air near a catwalk burst and a chunk came crashing down on Gillum's head. He was back to work in three hours. He smirked manfully at me when I asked him how he was. "That was the toughest triangular I ever had to put on," said Wigan. "Heads bleed. There was so much blood I couldn't see where the fucken cut was." Daily someone on the spreaders ran, hand to eye, blinking, streaming tears, to the eyewash, whose stream, like the drinking fountain's, was steadily yellowing.

HOW SAFE ARE YOU TODAY?

Jackson kicked out the dolly and on hands and knees rode it out and raised his back (!) too fast and stood into the elbow of the arm. I'd done that too. It dug in and scraped the skin off your spine. At any time a core layer's hand would bite backwards, the fingers curled, then snapping out, "Ouch, fuck, *sharp* up there. Hold it a fucking second." The glove would be peeled back with the teeth and the tiny wound, generally in the middle of the palm, inspected. Pale pink blood and glue circled the hole in the glove-liners. Trivial mishaps overrode the major dangers. The toggle-ends of my hydraulic lift-controls, when yanked on too hard, would dance in the air and when they began to fall back in their weight, and caught the edge of a travelling sheet, would be lashed out to their limit, way up near the shadow-line, and then made a nicely weighted plummet to hit me, stunningly hard, on the head.
"All I ever think about anymore is safety," said Wigan.

There were legendary and spectacular mill accidents that rendered the above insignificant. Two occurred while I was there. One was the crushing of Floyd's legs and the other was the return of the man who feared the drum sander and always wore underwear.

Once while wandering back from a piss break I jogged directly in front of Smith slowly rolling on the forklift. He began yelling and swearing at me. Stretch called me over. "He's telling you not to walk under the forks," he said. "It hasn't happened yet but if the lines give and the load drops, you're dead."

I met Floyd at the back of the mill near the grading line. I looked up from my hands and knees under the grader where I was shoving out sawdust and Mac's coffee cups and the big doors to the warehouse opened and Floyd came rolling in his hand up to grab the doorclose cord. He jumped off and came over to me hand extended. "Name's Floyd. Pretty soon it's Miller time. I gotta be back here in six hours. Damn glad to meet you."

We talked a bit.

"So you've been here as long as Süleyman?"

"Süleyman?' A nasty grin. "Süleyman? Yeah, he's been here long. We do make some mistakes here and he's one of them."

"Is this okay?" I said quickly.

"Yeah, sure, fuck the other day McMack sends that big kid Chuckles over here and he spends forty five minutes rolling around on his fat ass under there. Fuck he's lazy. His old man's here. Now he's trying to weasel his way in."

I just missed seeing it when the two lifts of 4.2 core fell on Floyd's legs. I did take note of the ambulance that showed up, and I did catch a glimpse of Floyd under a grey blanket on a stretcher. Rooney and I had to reload the fallen lifts. Because of this accident I participated in the only discussion I have ever had about a mannequin and the ordering, by way of sympathetic get-well-card group sponsorship, of an inflatable doll. My contribution to this discussion was, "I think I'm pretty sure there are a couple of places downtown you can get them. Sex shops."

"Some of our boys don't look so hot in McDonald's caps, you know."

This was one of the few quotes the plant manager offered to the local paper. He was trying to get sympathy and possible political support from an MLA because the mill had a problem with an inconsistent and overpriced log supply. I suppose we were being offered up as the threatened workers. What was it supposed to mean? Would we look that retarded serving French fries? Were we even capable of that? Did this comment appeal to my fellow grunts?

The other media statement he made, whose language revealed a level of contempt unusual from a man whose job was to sit in his hockey jacket and bark into telephones, "Yeah, well you'll let me know when something comes up won't you?", was in regards to dryer emission levels, which were so high and noxious as to warrant a warning from a committee. The statement?

"Pollution, what's pollution? Really, it's pretty clean."

Labonte had laid core for thirty five years and he was a character's character. His facial expressions were priceless, lathe-made. When he squinted at the rollers, looking for the next piece of core, his shoulders hunched and his hands in a staggered receiving stance, he looked like a parrot aping a pirate. "What's this?" he'd bark. "Watch the FLAP." "Lift those sheets straight up." "Over my head." "Get them off my back." He was ornery. He was mean. When he wanted his own way he got it, he laid up shit when he felt like getting ahead and took long breaks. He was raky. His Adam's Apple stuck way out. He was referred to, deferently, as a real ladies' man.

Core Feeding

Is a deck of cards you deal to the roller, right to left, is speed, is the name of the game is what you're doing is core feeding. Speed and the mirror. You are supposed to watch. For safety. For avoidance of blindness by puncture by what you are throwing at him. See his hands (?rorrim eht ni), they're his your target, corelayer, is who you're working with. Never look at him and he won't look at you. Is his yellow gloves that crabcrawl right to left. Shout anything you want at him, he has to catch the core. Only in the mirror. Feed core! Is I pump my deck up, jerk gluevalve open, in at the flap goes a broken corner, quickly spinflipped, artistically, come on unclip, unclip the other fingers, through, through, yes, core in the roller. Here's a flimsy fucker—whoosh. Scrap box. Is morecore, the last in the row (the gloves lay in the mirror, yellow maniacs in the glue speckles, lay and clutched on the brown, slick core). Is you are the edge of the impending sheet in the mirror, so you strop him a strip, and flash, the sheet whitens the mirror: my God! Yank shut the glue. Is core feeding is all day I tell you what I do is core feed, I watch the mirror.

Is— "What the hell you doing up here? Now I ask you. I mean are you having a bad day? Now here's how I want that core fed. You're leading; you set the pace. Are you having a bad day, you sometimes I know what it's like you stand up here all day and it's no fun. We're only human. Me—I like doing it."

Tabby was peeling core off the load and throwing it through the spreader as fast as he could. He fed like a crazy man.

"I mean we're just humans. I was watching you you're like Süleyman, he jaws away feeds the core all la de dah and then I come around he goes like hell. Now here. Now feed that core."

Stripe, stripe. It could be worse. Is I could be

Sheet turning

In which sometimes songs did it, the two hour stint. I knew an Arab torch song full of gutturals, but found that shouting it quickly pulled me off-key. Somehow the footwork required suited a rap. There were just enough steps back to the sheets for a quick couplet.

Polecat Boy-boy was down by the crick.

He was doing something wicked with a hickory stick.

Blast! went the arm, and the sheet plushed up, like a partridge, like a snowdrifted wind.

The sheet settled against the backboard, underslide, not a hint.

Hickory stick, you got to know.

Everybody giving it the old hi-ho.

"What the fuck you talking about?" said Wigan.

Old hi-ho, monkey on the back.

All going downtown never coming back.

Never coming back to a coldwater flat.

In the city, in the city,

Matter of fact.

Counter-attack.

Polecat came back with something kicking in a sack.

Polecat boy,

Whatcha got, boy?

Don't know paw, he's a kicking mighty mean.

Well we better. Affix him.

To the party machine.

The party machine, you got to know.

Got three speed settings, it ain't got a slow.

Look at him run,

110

Dynamo hum,
When he stick it in put your money on come.
Polecat sitting in the pale moonlight,
Paw and his pissing cup, pale moonlight,
Pa got an itch, Polecat the cure,
Took out the whip, said a prayer for the poor,
And lit into Paw.
Hur-rah.
Coffee.

As we walked to the lunchroom, Wigan turned to me and said, "I'm your master rapper and I'm here to say, that I dig fruity pebbles in a major way."

Gorlm, from Newfoundland, with his shaggy mop and mutt jaw under Case cap, slouched around on hot-patch for a few weeks. He said *fuck* a lot. He claimed every Monday to have shut down several bars——"and I was hucked clean out of the Colwood Corners, so's I decided to mosey down to the Forge and I shut her down and Laza here was near passed out. Hoo-wee, little chickie in the Forge, she was playing with my lighter and I said, Come on here and we'll teach you how to play with it."

"Yeah, and how's your old lady getting on with that guy drives pizzas?" said Laza.

"Babu? Fuck, I told her. This guy she knows him from before, but I fucking told her there's no way, he's a Hindu." Meaning his skin was darker than Gorlm's. "And he's been drinking with her. I'll fucking ba-boo him one of these nights."

That got him going.

Morning. I was hunching into one of those killer chills I got crossing the parking lot. I came into the lunchroom and ritually plugged the coffee machine, 35¢, coffee cream sugar extra strong. Listened to it pissing up the cup. The spreader crews were at the tables where we always sat, staring at the steam coming off their coffees, at the whisps of their cigarettes. Jeff came in. He sat down. "Guys."

"So, Jeff, did you go around to Craig's favorite hangouts?"

"Yeah, I had one drink at all of them. The Carlton. Champs."

He shook his head.

It sunk in.

"Was Craig in an accident?" I said.

111

"Dead," said Jeff.

After a bit someone said there was a witness and all he had seen was a ball of flame. Early Sunday morning Craig had gone off the road near Sooke—hit a power pole and the transformer had dropped on him. Incinerated him.

"I guess I'm feeding on number three today," said Jeff.

We got up and walked to our jobs.

Later on I learned that Jackson had been the last to see Craig alive. But he would not be the last to see Craig.

"Now the number one thing up here is to pay attention to what you're doing. Now I know you're smart, you're a university man" —I rolled my eyes, why had I ever told Tabby that—"so you're gonna work safe. Labonte had got hit between the eyes and fell over broke his arm. So watch the mirror. Pay attention what he's doing."

It was during one of Tabby's lectures that my dream-child of the mill, Stubby MacNamara, was born. I saw him enter, boots like sledges, at the warehouse doors. Stubby was one of the old school of sheet turners. They liked to come around and laugh at the sheet turners they had nowadays the little sissies in their cute white liners and their rubber gloves, like they were doing the dishes. When Stubby turned it was a man's world, and he was a man's man, sixteen, twenty-four hour shifts he turned with one hand, talking of horses and armature factories, of ten-penny nails found rusty in a weedy field. He chewed tobacco, no, he *ate* tobacco. Essentially Stubby was a Paul Bunyan figure. In my idle moments I polished tales of his presence, attributing to him spreader achievements, like the time he fed core, jumped down, laid it, turned the sheet and ran over now and then to load the press. He had done four-oh-three that day. I began to try out Stubby jokes and sayings on the crews.

Calum reacted in the most interesting manner. He turned the jokes back on himself and began to talk about others noticing or talking behind his back about his own slow pace. Stubby's feats didn't appeal to Calum's sense of humour at all. He was too deep within his own shit. Hyperconscious of performance, and of being ostracized, but never quite dedicated to performance, Calum would say, suddenly, with that phony wobbledy walk of his, *Aw, you know, the other day some of those guys were talking and, can you believe it, one of them actually said, you want to talk sheet turning, you shoulda been here ten years ago. Sheet turner, these guys now don't know the meaning of the word.* I was delighted. It was just the sort of thing Stubby would have said.

Calum was still whining: "And I thought, you know, this is getting ridiculous, it's like they actually believe it. Yup, they turned sheets a million, billion times better than us but I know, believe you me, we've been doing our jobs at a pretty fair pace. Yup. This time next year I'll be back at school."

After I left the mill I went to Calum's place to tell him to change his welfare mailing address—I was getting his mail because back in the summer, around the time of the fire layoff, he had asked me for the favour so he could get a hardship cheque sent but not to his place because his spouse was claiming welfare benefits already and it'll just be for this one thing, give a guy a break, eh.

But here it was nearly a year later and I was tired of calling him and ending up delivering his mail all the time. We talked. We watched an American sitcom, a principle action and laughtrack-activator of which was a father who did little but sit on a couch, perfectly deadpan, and produce twenty dollar bills from his pocket for his surly offspring, a standard vaudeville of the beaten-down. He was married to a hair-do in a pair of leopard tights. I looked into their kitchen at a dish of rindy margarine melting in a dirty dish.

"Well, anyway, I'd appreciate it if you changed the address. So, how's the mill?"

Then he did something that still surprises me when I think of it. He got this ferretty excited look in his eyes and whipped off his cap and pointed, jabbing, at his pate. "You see this?" he asked. He was angry, shaking-so. "I got a few years on some of those guys. I can do it, but it gets to the point where you know how it is, you just go in and do your job, you just, put, in your, eight hours. You just do your job. It's no contest. There's no prize!"

I stared at him and his penitent round scalp, astonished. The embarrassment I felt was sheer, repugnant. It was closely followed by anger. I inwardly said, *Yeah, well don't think we didn't notice it was just eight hours to you.* Jackson was right. What a dipshit. What a tremendous display of weakness.

I thought of the rindy butter.

Thoroughly human. What I said was, "Well, better apply for school, then." Prim. Ask yourself, who was the bigger asshole? I had to get out of there. I walked into a stench of burning rubber —great gouts of black smoke over the sidewalk, issuing from the half-drum of a barbecue. A man smoking a cigar with a bare

113

midriff was burning wire insulators and electric frying pan switches, a whole pile. It was a wonder he didn't asphyxiate himself. They didn't seem to be the sort of fuel that would completely burn down, either. Consequently, he was dousing them with lighter fluid and taking a step back when the drum bust upwards in swanky flames.

RECLIP

All of it had been, the men ascending in clouds to load the press, the dryer feeders endless in their placing of veneer ends to the infeed, except their cyclical repetitions were frozen, stuck together, needed to be shook then shunted in, the twinned figures and their one two steps back for the sheets, all *maya*—illusions—but to say it was to resemble the flower children, the backpacked and bearded, those who struck tents on damp hillsides at rainbow gatherings. Parents.

And the people you talk to on the telephone, the people you work with, even live with, you are merely adding, year after year, more and more images of yourself, of your creation, until you would never be free of it, you walk in the ruins of the past. I saw they had nothing to do with me. Season of airports! Nor I with them. It was worse: I *was* them. My problem, not theirs. And this is far more common than we think. Intimacy is rare. Things get said: rash, stupid. Judgments are made. The self is always quick to eradicate the reality of another.

The Raimann patchers used to blow off their pedestal-sized carpets at the end of shift, and the football-shaped fir chips scattered in tracking patterns on the floor. Then they blew off their clothes and hair, waxed their tables bright, found their coats, and left.

Wigan said it one day, not me. He should get the credit. He said, really what this place is is a bunch of machines and a few people running around trying to keep the machines happy. But when he said it, I recalled Wigan spent most of his weekends on watch when the machines weren't running, and he knew that the mill was a terrific home for swallows with its struts and catwalks and dark, high ceilings, and he used to see them whizzing far above the press platforms, late at night, when it was cold, on watch, weekends.

One foggy evening I went back to the mill. It was midnight, drizzly, the clouds revealing a clear full moon. I stood outside my parked car and looked into where between dryers number two and three someone's legs then full figure walked away, enwrapped and unwrapped in voluptuous stained steam. My hand reached for another cigarette.

The click and hiss of the infeed.

I was ready again.

Chambers saw the Kid wasn't looking and he took the Kid's broom and hurled it in a whooshing spin way up over the lifts and out the bright panel of window at the roofline. He whooped, and spanked his gloves together.

"Pretty good shot, eh?"

His grin was an entire Cheshire.

WHAP WHAP WHAP

"Feed the fucking core, homo."

"Aw you fucking homo yourself, here."

In the fall that year Labonte was sick, then stayed sick, was away from his job for better than a month. There were rumours. People claimed to have seen him staggering at this or that mall or bingo palace. There was speculation whether he'd return. I never saw it, if he has. Wigan thought the glue had got to him. Disturbed his equilibrium. Or perhaps he had drunk himself to death—that one floated out of the general conversation without much comment one day.

Sometimes I'd be driving past the entrance to the mill when the shift changed and I could see them, for an instant, in their cars, in a long line, each face behind the windshield, the grimness, the fatigue, the drifting, the left turn, the lights, the way they left the mill in their vehicles. At approximately the same time. But I never could make Cowboy appear again, in his Rambler, clutching his redoubtable thermos, any more than I could stop Craig up in the core-feeder's platform, stop the glint off his glasses from reoccurring. I just couldn't do that. Sorry.

<u>Two Rooms</u>

Terry hardly ever went out. This had

been his practise in other cities and it was his practise in this one. He had up and left his job and come here spending almost all of his real estate settlement on drugs, and stayed, spending a good deal of his rent and food money on drugs, living in an apartment he could see every bit of from his sofa. The apartment seemed to him an extension of his body; the only question mark was the door barring the bathroom. He was soon forced into an unenergetic mode which he was used to. He thought eventually he would find a job, perhaps at a convenience store, and make just enough money to get by and now and then buy more drugs and relax, kick back. But UI was only so much money and it went fast. He had to think of the video games he wanted to rent and the movies.

It was necessary to make a few economies, so he began to get up early in the morning, while it was still dark, and walk through the business district looking for cigarette butts, which he collected in a plastic bag. He felt noble about this, big enough to do it, that sort of thing. Through the day he would smoke rerolled cigarettes slowly, taking an half hour a cigarette. He operated his games-controller with one hand while he rolled them.

On the few other occasions Terry was outside he noticed that it rained a lot and there were many old people living here. He had a couple of people over, friends of friends, to smoke a joint and Terry remarked that these senior citizens seemed scared when he approached them on the sidewalks. They seemed to think he was young, burly and dangerous. Terry's acquaintances agreed politely with him: old people were more concerned about safety and crime these days.

When they left, Terry knew they had thought him ridiculous, hardly dangerous at all.

He lived on Kraft dinner and oatmeal, sometimes rice, an egg. He cooked everything in a wok, to save on cooking implements and make one more repetitive process out of the days. He imperfectly cleaned the wok when he felt like it. He drank what liquids he could afford out of empty pop-bottles.

Terry picked up the phone.

"Hello, Ron?"

"Yeah, how's it going, guy?"

"I was just about to go down to McDonald's."

"Aw, no, man, you don't wanna do that." Ron tamped his

cigarette. He watched cars slide by. "Still there? Listen, I can do you a front till next Friday. How's that?"

"Okey-dokey."

"Be there by six."

"Why thank you, sir."

Terry returned his attention to the TV. It was always on. He liked the unity. It all added up and poured forth there. Actors had been cast for their striking resemblance to dead and famous flesh. The sideburned teens Terry saw showing up at their girlfriends' houses had the pallor of past decades grained in them, speeding coupes, famous intersections. Sloping, cunning camera angles, cut, cut, shadows and actors. Rallies were staged for soft drinks. Names called out to names. Max Headroom a design-feature-cum-emblem, a martial whippersnapper. He envisioned a sitcom about a couple with a child named Factory Air. It had all been done before, the Ramayana, cops on duty turning from the steering wheel to adlib the mini-cam. Left-crossing, right-crossing, legspring, the black and white tribes of the world wore the colours of the sun, of faded denim, sunlight on brownstone and beer bottle, sunlight on running water, sunlight on drinking glasses and citrus groves, on dog-pelt. Game show sets were like talk-show sets were like science fiction sets were like electronic town-hall meetings. He grinned slyly when the word democracy came out of the set. In the daytime personalities whose hair he loved delved deeper into the deep sordidity of the interpersonal. These were his guides to estrangement, sexual confusion, betrayal, bigotry. Hosting your horror we'll be right back. I think we all learned something today. We did? Terry remembered an interview with an interviewer who confessed that he needed all the perks of stardom; otherwise he just couldn't keep going. Terry found this touching. His river of sleep and song.

Long after Ron had left and they had smoked and coughed their lungs out over the sink, the screen lost its resolution; characters there seemed forlorn suddenly, distant, trapped behind the glass in a slight visual static. Terry realized the sun had gone down.

He drew the curtains.

Sat down.

"Kick back," he said.

"Re. Lax."

He switched from station to station.

His headrest on the couch was near a thin wall separating his head from the outside door: when the cook upstairs got off his shift, and opened the door, Terry tensed, aware the intruder's legs and body were very near his head. He curled up tighter, until he heard the steps going upstairs. Sometimes, sufficiently stirred from sleep, he'd sit up and switch the TV on again and let the switching light from the screen play against his eyes. He shivered constantly, had to take deeper and deeper breaths. No one there now. One other who made noise in the room—his heart, which he would meet some day.

One day Terry went downtown to buy hash at McDonald's. He ignored the skate-boarders, and waited until the usual kid came over. Then they went for a walk.

"So, what do I owe you?" Terry said.

The kid reached out with the burnt-off baggie and said, "Fifteen", and dropped it on the sidewalk. Terry's hand hadn't been there. He reached down for it, to correct his error, and the kid stepped on his hand. Terry cried out, and pushed the kid over, kicked him in the head. He kicked him in the head again.

The kid didn't move.

Blood appeared at the side of his mouth.

Terry tried to move him but he proved to be heavier than he thought. He was at the entrance to a parking garage. He dragged the kid inside. The elevator. The basement. Terry hurried. The elevator doors opened on a couple. It was quite impossible to disguise what had happened. They ran away. Terry closed the door again, pushed buttons. It rose one. The door opened to a cop.

"Going down?" said Terry.

His mother showed up at the holding centre just before Terry's sentencing. His father wouldn't come. Terry thought she might be concealing an object to attack him with—but no, that was how she generally held her purse, he remembered, under her coat. She wore a poppy for some reason and the coat bespoke wartime industry. Something was funny about her hair. Had she removed a showercap?

"Mom," he said.

"Don't you *mom* me now look what you've gone and done the boy not twenty years old your father is an old man now and don't say we didn't try and raise you right, properly."

"Okay." Terry shrugged.

119

"Don't give me that."

As he studied the connections, the dense optic web of salute and reference presented, the stars of other shows appearing tonight, the jokes and jibes at other entertainers, the appearance-swapping where the reincarnation of earlier loved faces were new talent, the backslapping, the cartoon characters who populated advertisements, and above all the myriad times people on TV watched TV, the screens smaller and smaller (like Alice's porthole in the grass) he saw it was essentially one thing he was watching, one imprint, nostalgically engineered to treasure only the lovable, happy fools living on credit and taking hikes with tubs of margarine. Dogs were loved. Anyone who had ever fallen down a flight of steps was loved. Dirt was thoroughly cleansed. Parents thoughtfully dosed children with drugs in a soft-focus pity. Other, more deadly diseases were the scourge of celebrities, one more reason to strike it up, show clips, rescue the voice and the face and get it out there one last time. The screen's howling against death. Its infinite memoria.

He could sleep again.

He begins (he thinks) to have a dream of a blackened hand pressing towards his face. Through its fingers are lit human figures, beyond. The hand keeps pressing and pressing on his face.

Treeline

Jerry noticed the treeline that year,

when it was sufficiently dark. How many thousand feet. He just noticed it, that's all.

He told his friends when they phoned from Ontario—university friends—he was a reporter on a weekly, the words still had a certain fourth year élan, in Northern B.C. His friends were lodged somewhere in a mounting pyramid of Ottawa acronyms. Over the three years there had been fewer calls. His parents lived on the Lower Mainland; he visited them on his holidays, which he usually took in August and derived an almost sexual thrill from the iced fish and the Greek pastries and the glowing produce at Granville Island market. Beautiful women in sunglasses were all over, buying croissants and molded nutbreads. He ate a lot of fries and burgers in Kwalitum. He was chunky, definitely, or perhaps it was the sweatshirts he wore under his only sports jacket when he had to cover meetings.

"Things going all right?" his editor said to him now and then. He meant, Are you doing your job, Will You Be Requiring That I Interrupt My Drinking? The editor stepped circumspectly around the desks on his way to the door, then lowered his voice to a near-whisper, "I'll be at the Crest." Jerry thought this childish. He was right. The editor did do a number of things in his spare time that would have widened Jerry's eyes.

Jerry avoided the Crest. He couldn't tolerate their long-winded discussions about what land was most grabbable and how far out of town it was and wouldn't some sucker from Vancouver pay a bundle for it. Recently in Kwalitum a distantly removed branch of a business-gospel ring that also carried overtones of men's reawakening had started up and it attracted all those approaching fartdom: the used car peddler, the real estate man, the stereo shop owner. Instead of banging drums they gathered in the Crest and palmed salty peanuts, talked incessantly of money, women, taxes. The Gospel aspects were wholly confined to their brunches. Scrambled eggs, some laying on of hands, a brief talk by a chain-smoker about feeling the spirit. Then back to drinking. Pigs in blankets. They had invited him once, and he had a hard time making conversation, and left, incredulous. People had no idea what they sounded like when they started telling their meticulously crafted but poorly performed versions of their lives. No idea.

122

Jerry had very little idea himself. He was always surprised when he suffered his own feelings——the gang at the Crest had rebuffed him in many ways. This made him angry. They had a sort of humour-the-young-pup attitude towards him and it came out once when McWean, the heating-king, had commented on Jerry's lack of luck with women. "Guess it must be frustrating, slim pickings around these parts. Jerry, you don't look like you're trying very hard."

This was, unfortunately, true.

His woodstove-containing A-frame, about as unrustic as something pre-fab near a powerline could be, filled with expendable and eventually ignored toys. When he didn't feel like doing much he rented movies from the gas-station, stayed in, watched the snow fall and cooked himself rudimentary stews.

He had a certain ambulation in the town, a routine, meaning he knew where stories were likely to be available, in which buildings, or shuffled out and handed over in the cab of a four-by-four. By the predictable people. If the stories got too large his sources in town became silent. He placed a call. He waited. He wrote something else.

One of the nurses had condescended to date him a while ago because he had been persistent. She did little to disguise her impatience; Jerry sensed he was something that would happen to her before she left. And that, except for an evening in bed with her, was what happened. While they made love, Jerry was anxious; but as soon as they were finished, she leapt up and went to sit in front of the woodstove. What had he done?

Already she was somewhere else; he could see that.

"Sometimes these things hurt," she said.

Alarmed, Jerry said quickly, "It's too soon to be thinking about that kind of thing. We just—"

"No. No, I mean I hurt. Here. Jesus."

For a reporter, Jerry was incurious about what people talked about over coffee. He never tried to eavesdrop. He was afraid he would hear his name. "Jerry? He doesn't know shit-all."

But how exciting it had been when green, the fresh notepads, the pens, the paper's beater to take three miles up the river, the twisting road, what little he knew about the local band repeating and distorting in his head. Native fishing. He parked and walked a ways to the river, just down from a weir. Gradually along the path the leaves were replaced by a lone man sitting on the bank with an electronic device. *Hey,* Jerry went. *Shhh,* signalled the man. Jerry was nearing him when something exploded; the sky whirled; he dropped, felt wet. The man was above him, gripping the electronic box, offering his other hand. "Ancient knowledge of my fucking people, eh?"

Then he had started to collect the dead fish.

There was someone he was interested in, and she was a secretary at the comprehensive school. Earlene her name was. He judged her to be about his age, perhaps older. Education was part of his beat, and probably where he got the majority of his stories. Through Earlene he had access to the principal, a brutal-looking man, soft-spoken and with a scale model of a Porsche on his desk. There was rarely anything else on his desk. Earlene set up the interviews with him and took Jerry's neatly typed questions to the principal. By the time Jerry got there, he just took down the man's banal replies. Still, even to the most balloonish statement from provincial education authorities, the man would make sensible sounding predictions; and he even, through Earlene, handed Jerry a few modest scoops. Suddenly released funds for renovation of a gymnasium. New program written up as innovation in *The Surrey Journal of Primary Studies*. He kept coming back.

Earlene wore dark makeup, darker than anyone's he'd seen, though she was fairish, her hair a mousey muddling colour. She wore Reebok cross-trainers with her dresses.

"What are those," Jerry had said once, pointing to a plastic bag.

"My high heels," she said.

He never pressed her. She always smiled at him. Never did he feel he was another task to be gotten through. But he never felt he knew her either. Perhaps that was why his attention towards her took a long time to build into anything decisive. He knew things about her: the way she replaced the plastic cover on her keyboard and the way she lifted it. The way she would try to get one finger underneath her watchband and twist, when distracted. Little things. She was a source. She loved a dirty joke and supplied them because he could never remember jokes.

They had done it facing each other, pulled each other's triggers with strings and big toes, a contraptive uneasiness about which he dreaded, because it reminded him crisply of a children's game called mousetrap.

124

He left the schoolyard in the middle of recess. He walked through the children, aware of their own wariness. A girl skipped out of his way dragging a plastic cowbell in a clunkedy circle around her ankle. Others hopping over bouncing superballs near the brick wall stopped hopping, watched him until he was beyond the fence. A boy made an obscene gesture at him and punched the tetherball which wound up the pole, jerked, and started to unwind down.

He had been tricked. How could he have known? There was an implausibly black and purple sill she lived behind; a pulse in the purse of an onionskin. Her bruisy makeup. She loved a dirty joke. He had kept coming to her—source. She let him know things well in advance. Granted him access to the principal.

Jerry and his editor and a few of the Crest gang sat at the back in the funeral home when the service for the principal happened. None of them were quite sure what to expect. Hardly anyone was there. For the others, thought Jerry, who recognized most of the furniture in the room from other, earlier failed businesses, the entire town must seem a collection of hardware to be disassembled and set up again in other configurations as time passed.

If they had expected something in poor taste to occur, they were not disappointed. A man no more than four foot six showed up, and, after shaking hands a rather long time with the staff person, proceeded to offer a few words as an elegy. When he turned to face them they were shocked to perceive he looked remarkably like a monkey. Incredibly, he started his speech with a few words about himself, a figure he was not able to eliminate from his remarks entirely. "Jack was born in England, he never did have the great fortune that I did to be born in Scotland, but we both came to the admirable city of Victoria after the war and by God, we were successful, he and I, and his children were successful." Here the monkey stepped back from the lectern as though to let his audience see the fine suit he wore. "And so, through God's great fortune, we became colleagues and rivals in the insurance game. Why—"

The editor had laughed.

"Why many's the time Jack and I would have lunch together at the finest restaurants and make pleasant conversation about the passing scene, though we worked for different companies. Often I'd be on the phone to Toronto, and would say, Say, I had lunch with Jack Jamieson today, and they wouldn't have it, Oh no, they'd go, he's the competition, and I'd say You just don't understand the way things are out here in British Columbia. Yes, Jack and I were two of a kind, and when we parted, I made my own way, as he did, among the towns and people of this great province, always trusting that the Lord would continue to be good to us. I want to fondly remember the many games of golf we enjoyed." The monkey spoke well, with a thunderous intonation, for more than twenty minutes. After the first while Jerry had sat increasingly tense, increasingly angry, surely this was a joke? Well, what are you doing here?

When the monkey finished he made a point of coming back and shaking their hands. Jerry noticed he wore tartan socks. They saw him last at the exit, thumbing through a tiny datebook.

"That little shit was quite something, eh. What do you say, Jerry, coffee?"

"Sorry, I've got things to do."

Earlene's face appeared to him in the next week often, the only fresh sign undeteriorated from what had been a highly coherent dream.

There she was again.

After all, we both worked in the same small town.

A rising vase of white flesh, her neck with the lightest blue veins when she wore black. Adjusted her swivel-seat height. He had known her for years, known her lipstick cycles, knew nothing about her. Years she had put aside her knitting, when she had some, or a vapid magazine to chit-chat with him.

One night he drove out to the address he had for her. He parked in front of an ugly brown split level in the Small Mountain development. It had an old deck. After a while a light went on in the front entrance and a man in a dressing-gown scampered out to him.

"You better leave or I'll call the police."

"Okay, I'm leaving."

He drove down the mountain, slowly. Compulsively he kept checking the rear-view.

He stopped at the dump and unfocused his eyes on a chain link fence and sat, exhausted, until he made out the blinking red beacon at the airport, then turned on the car again. *I've got to get out of here*, Jerry said.